WIFED BY A BOSS

MS. KEENA

TEXT UCP TO 22828 TO SUBSCRIBE TO OUR MAILING LIST
If you would like to join our team, submit the first 3-4 chapters of
your completed manuscript to
Submissions@UrbanChapterspublications.com

ACKNOWLEDGMENTS

Thank you, thank you, thank you to everyone that took the time out to purchase this book and all my other books. You guys don't know how nerve-wracking it was worrying if you guys would like it.

To my heartbeats, you are a reflection of me, so it's only right that I show you that anything can be accomplished with motivation. I hope that I am the inspiration that you seek when times get tough.

To my love, my best friend, and my biggest supporter, Charles, it only gets better. All the trials and tribulations will finally pay off as long as we stay strong together.

Tura, thank you for pushing me, believing me even when I didn't believe in myself, and always rooting for me. You are the definition of loyal and real as they come.

To my readers, thank you for your continued support. You guys gave me the push I needed with the numerous inboxes, comments, and reviews.

To my family, both near and far, thank you for the calls, texts, and support of ordering books. It's because of your support through word of mouth and sharing post on Facebook that these books have a success.

Follow me: @theauthorkeena
Instagram:theauthorkeena
Facebook: Sakina Walker& Author Keena
Facebook Author Page: Author Keena
Reading Group: Sakina Sensational Readers

1

_____

Asha

"Welcome to Miller's Steakhouse. My name is Asha and I will be your server for the night. Would you like to order a drink while you wait for the rest of your party?" I asked.

"Yeah, let me get a bottle of Louie XIII and a bottle of Grey Goose." He closed his menu and handed it to me.

"Okay, I'll be right back with your bottles."

I was working a party of fifteen tonight and was wondering why, of all nights, I was doing it alone. Usually, I wouldn't mind doing large parties by myself because the tips were amazing but, tonight, I was tired as hell. I had been working two jobs for the last nine months since I moved out of my Grandma's old house. Her house had gone into foreclosure before her passing a couple years ago. I would've loved to keep the house, but I couldn't because of Kandi's ass.

My mother wanted to fight me in court about everything that my grandmother had left me. Like she had money to pay legal fees, knowing she was barely paying her bills. I found it funny that she wasn't there to take care of my grandmother or even see her the months before her passing, but she was front and center when my grandmother finally passed, wanting people to feel sorry for her. The house wasn't left to me, but I was living in it.

She wanted to take everything that meant something to me away, including the car that my grandmother was driving. I let her have her jewelry only to find out that she went and pawned it. I was able to purchase it back because Grandma Dot and Mr. Greene were friends, so he gave me a deal on her stuff. Luckily, my friend Monica's mother was a lawyer and told me the best thing to do was to have the bank put the house up for sale, so I went forward with that.

I carried the bottles that were requested to the table and seated the rest of his party. I looked around and I could tell that this was going to be an interesting night. All the chicks that were seated around the table had bad weaves and couldn't dress worth a damn. I paid close attention to the gentleman who ordered the bottles and the chick that sat next to him. He was light skinned with a Ceaser cut that was graced with deep beautiful waves. He was built, so I could tell that he worked out often. The tattoos that covered his body were simply gorgeous. He wore a single chain around his neck, but it made a statement. The girl, on the other hand, was something ratchet with bundles from the beauty supply store and long nails with rhinestones on them. The worst part of her appearance were those damn butterfly lashes that you could tell Ling-Ling did. It looked like if she blinked three times her ass would fly away.

"Is everyone ready to order?" I asked.

"Yes, they are," he spoke up for everyone.

I went around the table and got everyone's order until I got to the chick sitting beside this fine-looking man. I was waiting for this one.

"Ummm, yea…let me get the skrimps and the fries," she requested.

While shaking his head at her, he began to place his order. "Let me get the seventeen-ounce rib eye with loaded baked potatoes, mushrooms and onions on the side."

After taking everyone's order, I went to enter it in the system so it could be cooked. Kayla walked over to me and started entering her orders.

Excitedly, she asked, "Girl, do you know whose party you are serving back there?"

"Umm, no... Who is it?" I questioned.

"Girl, that is Budah and his crew back there." She smiled so hard I was sure her cheeks were hurting.

"So, who is he?" I asked. I was confused. I could tell he had power from the looks of it, but I didn't know much about the guy.

"Girl, you have to get out more. He and his crew have all of the hoods on lock," she replied.

"How you know who he is and you're younger than I am?"

"Well, if your ass would go out once in a while instead of working all the time like an old lady, you would know something," she stated, and I laughed.

"Chile, these bills damn sure won't pay themselves. I got to do what I got to do."

Going back into the party room, I suddenly became nervous. Here I was in the presence of one of the most known bosses and didn't even know it. After I checked on them to make sure that everything was fine, I watched him and paid close attention to his every move.

When he looked up and saw that I was watching him, he smirked at me. I felt embarrassed so, instead of standing there in a weird space, I strutted towards the kitchen to check on their orders. The first order that was put in arrived. It was the food for the girl that was with Budah and her crew. As I placed the food in front of the chick with Budah, she had the nerve to catch an attitude. I tried to ignore her until her complaint became louder.

"Is everything okay with your order?" I asked in the politest way possible.

"Don't more skrimp come with this?" She frowned and picked through her food.

She looked disgusted with her order. It looked delicious to me, but she wasn't feeling it at all.

"No, ma'am, that is all that comes with your order," I told her.

The whole time that I was talking, Budah had his eyes on me, waiting to see how I would deal with her ass. I knew for a fact that I had to play it cool.

"All this money that my man is spending and you mean to tell me that this is all that I get? Y'all tripping!" She pushed the plate to the side and sipped from her fine wine glass.

"If you would like to order an additional side of shrimp, I can put an order in for you."

"Nah, go 'head on, sweetheart. You straight," Budah spoke.

I walked back to the kitchen with the plate and gently sat it on the counter. I leaned over the sink and counted to ten so I wouldn't snap on her rude ass when I went back to the front. Everyone else was fine with their orders and didn't say a word, but I wasn't surprised that she did the most. She acted just how she looked, a hot ass mess. When I was walked back out front, I looked in the direction of Budah and his lady. It was clear as day that she had an attitude, but that didn't stop him from looking at me with that sexy ass grin of his face. I couldn't control the blush that crept on my face. His stares did something to me.

This was the last party of the night, so the front of the restaurant was beginning to close. I went up front to help so that we could close sooner. I had to head to my second job as soon as I left this one. The second I turned around, I bumped right into Budah's strong chest.

"I'm so sorry," I quickly apologized.

"No apologies needed. I wanted to come and apologize for ole girl actions. If she would've read the menu, she would've known how many she was getting. What's your name?" he asked.

"Asha," I told him.

"Nice to meet you. I'm Budah." He extended his hand, and I shook it. "We should be ready back there if you want to bring me the bill." He turned to walk away.

We both made our way back into the room so that I could get their bill and prepare to clean their table. As soon as we walked into the room, Budah's chick immediately started with her drama and antics.

"I know damn well you aren't trying me with this busted ass chick!" she yelled at Budah, causing a scene.

I turned my head to see who she was talking about because I knew for a fact that she couldn't have been talking about me. I continued to look around the room as if I was lost, and Budah burst out in a loud laugh. He thought that I was playing, but I really wanted to know who the fuck she was talking about.

"Yeah, you!" she yelled.

She came around the table as if she was about to do something, but Budah stopped her before she reached me.

"Man, chill out with all of that." Budah held her arm.

"Ain't no chill, you really trying me with this chick!" she screamed, causing a big scene.

Angrily, he said, "Let's wrap this shit up before I fuck around and fuck this dumbass bird up. You have been showing your ass since you walked into this restaurant."

I finished cleaning the tables and a couple of the bus boys, Josh and Markus, were there to help me as well. Budah walked back into the area, scaring the hell out of me.

"How is it that you move so quietly?" I asked him.

"Killers move in silence," he said then laughed. "Nah, for real, this is for tonight," he said, handing me five one hundred-dollar bills.

I smiled and fingered through the cash. "Thank you. I really appreciate this."

"What you about to get into? "He jumped straight to the point.

"I'm off to my second job when I leave here."

"Oh okay. Well, don't work too hard." He smiled and left.

Lord knows it had been hard for me since my grandmother passed a couple years back. She was my rock and the one I would run to for any and everything. She was damn near my mother. She raised me like I was hers even with my mother living a couple minutes away from us. My grandmother felt that Kandi wasn't ready to take care of me, especially since she had a habit of doing drugs. My grandmother had come to the house on more than one occasion and saw that I was there alone with no food and no one to care for me. The final straw was when a neighbor called my Grandma Dot and told her that I had been home alone for three days and my mother hadn't been there to check on me at all. That was the last night that I ever lived with Kandi.

It was no secret that she felt like Jerry was the reason my mother started doing drugs because he was on them. Jerry wasn't my father. He was Kandi's boyfriend but he never mistreated me, so I didn't have an issue with him. She tried to get herself clean a few times, but she never succeeded. She would be clean for weeks, sometimes months, then fall victim to the crack pipe all over again.

I thought that everything would change when she had my little sister, but that didn't happen. She did well, all the way up until Justice was about twelve years old, then she went back to her same old ways. She tried to hide it from us because she knew that my grandmother would snatch Justice just how she had done me. So, when she would come around us, she was always on her best behavior.

When my grandmother passed, I tried to help my mom out with my sister but she was so negative that I just kept in contact with Justice and stopped talking to my mother altogether. She really was in her feelings when I received a check from my grandmother's life insurance policy. I guess she figured since she was my grandmother's daughter she would get the money from the policy instead. She didn't talk to me for damn near a year because of it.

I had thoughts of calling out tonight from my second job at XS since Budah had left me such a large tip. I had made enough to cover my rent and car payment with the rest of the money that I already had.

2

BUDAH

I don't even know why I still fuck with Ameka's ass. She wasn't my type. The only thing that she wanted to do was ride around with me and try to convince everyone that she was my lady, which was not the case. Ameka didn't have any of the qualities that my mother or aunt had, and that was what I was looking for in someone that I wanted to share my world with.

Case in point, tonight at the restaurant. The bitch acted a fool about some damn shrimp. If I would've known she was going to act like that, her ass could've gone to the seafood store and ordered a basket of her own. Then, she had the nerve to show her ass at the restaurant. I hated when people acted like they came from money and started acting brand new when, in fact, they didn't have a pot to piss in or a window to throw it out. I was deep in thought when I pulled up to her spot.

"So, you're not going to say anything about what happened at the restaurant?" She looked at me with an attitude and her arms crossed.

"Look, I'm not in the mood to be playing with you. You chose to show your ass for no damn reason back there." I pointed behind me.

"So, you coming back after the club?"

"Nah, I'm cool. In fact, I'm going to fall back from you before I have to snap your fucking neck!"

"Really, Budah? You tripping!" She shook her head then opened the door to get out.

Once I pulled off, I headed to Club XS where we were going to be celebrating my dude, Sham. He was just released after doing a long and hard bid. He was the true definition of loyal. When the pressure fell on him, he didn't fold. In fact, he stood in the paint and served his time like a G and, for that, he could get whatever he wanted from me.

When I arrived, the crew was waiting for me. I got out the car and all of us headed inside the club. We were immediately seated in the V.I.P. section it was already set up for us with bottles and chaser. The hostess what waiting on us to arrive once we did she got us settled and left. The fellas were enjoying themselves, throwing money and hollering at the bitches while I sat back and relaxed.

I was waiting on the hostess to come back so that I could order a couple more bottles. She finally came back but, this time, it was a different person. It was the chick Asha from the restaurant. She had on a pair of thigh-high boots and a corset top with some short ass shorts to top the outfit off.

"Hello, I'm Asha, and I'll be serving you tonight. What can I get for you?" she greeted our table without even looking up.

"We meet again," I laughed.

She looked up at me and smiled. "Are you stalking me or something?"

"Nah, we were here first. I think you're stalking me," I replied.

"Here you go with the jokes. What can I get y'all?" she asked.

"Just run back what we already have here," I told her.

"Well, damn, didn't we just see you?" Rico asked.

"Yep, got to pay these bills," she said to him.

"Asha, tell the boss you are fucking with us tonight and take a seat." Rico waved his cup.

"Nah, I'm straight. Besides, I don't want to have to kick your lady and her crew's ass tonight," she said, making a nigga laugh.

Everyone laughed, but I could tell that she was dead ass serious by the expression on her face.

"Nah, you straight. I took her ass home." I shrugged.

"Okay, well, I'm going to be back with your bottles shortly." She turned on her heels and quickly walked away.

The entire time I watched her move around the club. She stopped a couple times to talk to a few people and served her other tables. The fellas partied and brought random chicks to our section, but my focus was on Asha. She was a thick girl with hips and thighs but was the baddest thing walking in the club. That was sexy to me; just her confidence alone turned me on.

We partied all night, and I continued to watch Asha throughout the night. As the club lights came on, we sat and waited for everyone to leave the club. I hated crowds. Shit always went wrong with crowds. Once we made it outside, we leaned against our cars and talked shit for a while. I was scrolling through my phone to see who I could slide into tonight but my luck was slim to none. All the bitches that were on my list were old, tired, and boring as fuck.

When I looked up, all the ladies from the bar and the servers were walking out of the club. I didn't say anything as I sat back and watched Asha interact with everyone she encountered. She was laughing and clowning around with them until they all said their goodbyes and went to their cars. My eyes followed her as she made her way to the car that was parked across from mine. When she tried to start her car, it didn't turn over. She tried a couple more times then put her head on the steering wheel.

I walked over to her to check and see if everything was okay. She was in the car damn near in tears.

"You straight, shorty?" I leaned down and asked her.

"My damn car isn't starting, and I can't figure out what is going on with it," she sniffled.

"Well, it's too late to try to figure it out. Grab your things and I'll talk you home." I smiled at her.

"If it's too much trouble, I can get an Uber," she replied.

"It isn't, let's ride." I walked back to my car and, soon, she followed me.

Telling the crew I'd holla at them later, Asha and I bounced. We rode and listened to the music as her phone continuously went off. I had a feeling that it was an important call, but she didn't want to be rude and answer while in the car with me. She looked down at her screen then said that it was her sister and she would call her when she got home. She lived about fifteen minutes away from the club, in the projects. I pulled in front of her apartment and turned off the car.

"So, where your nigga at?" I asked her.

"Who said I have one of those?" She smiled at me.

"Come on, you too sexy not to have a nigga."

"Well, if you must know, I do not have a dude."

I was about to say something to her but her phone went off again. This time she went ahead and answered it.

"Yes, Justice!" she yelled into the phone.

She was silent for a couple of minutes then responded to whomever Justice was. "I'll be over there tomorrow after I get my car looked at." She hung up the phone without so much as a goodbye.

"Everything straight?" I asked her.

"Yeah, just the usual bullshit at Jerry and Kandi's house," she responded.

"What does that mean?" I asked.

"Kandi is my mother and Jerry is her boyfriend. When I say the usual, they get drunk and want to fight. It's either about some money, who drank the last beer or something like that. Anyway, thank you for going out of your way to bring me home." She smiled and opened the door.

"No problem at all. Slide me your number so I can get your car sent over to you in the morning."

"That's fine, pass your phone. Make sure your guard dog doesn't get a hold of my number," she stated.

After putting her number in my phone, she exited the car. I watched her strut up the walkway to her apartment. She had the baddest walk that I had ever seen. It was enough to make my man stand at attention. When she safely got in the house, I went ahead and pulled off. I was thinking about going back to Ameka's house, but I didn't feel like dealing with the bullshit or hearing her mouth. The only thing she was good for was the sloppy head that she offered a nigga.

I decided to go home although a nigga was getting tired of going home to an empty house and a cold bed. I pulled into my house and admired the motherfucker. I had to admit, it was nice as hell for me to have built it myself. It was a five-bedroom, seven bathroom mini-mansion with a four-car garage. In the backyard, I had a huge Olympic-size pool with a hot tub and a fire display at the end where it gave an infinity drop-off look.

I had yet to break this house in properly. The only people that had come here to visit were my brother, little sister, my aunt, Tez, and Blaze. Business had been good, so it was only right that I took care of myself. I had been in the game since I was about eighteen and I humbly worked my way up to the top.

My crew supplied just about everything. Anything that anybody wanted, we had it or could get it. I invested into a couple businesses early on to make things look legit to the IRS and other eyes although I didn't lift a finger at all.

3

ASHA

Budah thought his ass was slick when he implied he needed my number for my car. I was told that he watched my every move tonight while I worked. I sat on the front porch, replaying everything from last night as I watched the bad ass kids play in the dirt. Their mother was so busy in a nigga's face that she didn't even see them. I had been working twelve days straight so I was glad that I would be off for the next three days from both jobs. I was tired as hell and didn't wake up until eleven o'clock this morning. I was about to call my sister when my phone began to beep, letting me know that I had a text.

Unknown: You up?

Me: Who the hell is this?

Unknown: Calm down with the attitude. It's way too early ma.

Me: Why didn't you just say that it was you in the first place?

Unknown: Be that way in 20 mins so get dressed. A nigga hungry.

I looked at the phone like I was crazy. This nigga didn't ask; he just told me what to do. I flew my ass into the house to find me something to wear though. I wrapped my hair last night so the only thing I had to do once I freshened up was flat iron it. I stepped into the shower and washed my body with my favorite body wash. Once I was done show-ering, I applied lotion all over my body. I wanted to be comfortable because it was hot as hell out and I didn't want anything hugging me today. I slipped into a long maxi dress and decided to dress it up with a pair of earrings and a gold chain with the matching bangles. I stepped into my sandals and walked into my bathroom to unwrap my hair that hung to the middle of my back. I was all natural and didn't need bundles or any other hair weave if I didn't want it. After I applied my lip gloss, Budah sent a text letting me know that he was pulling up. I stepped outside and locked my front door. Budah was leaning on his 2018 hunter green Range Rover looking sexy as hell. He was dressed in some all-white Gucci shorts and a white Gucci shirt with the Gucci loafers to match.

I walked up to him and realized he was on the phone with some-one, giving them instructions to text him when my car was ready. As I hopped into his truck, I relaxed in the passenger seat. I dug into my bag to find my shades. Once my shades were on my face, I buckled my seatbelt and prepared to ride with the boss.

Budah drove for about fifteen minutes before either of us said anything. I was nervous as hell. I couldn't speak for him though.

"Why you so quiet?" Budah asked me.

"I'm just enjoying the view and listening to the music," I told him and nodded my head to the old R&B.

He passed me the remote and told me to find something to listen to. He had Pandora playing so I selected Silk radio. The music was smooth and mellow.

"So, you like slow music?" He looked at me and smiled.

"Yea, I listen to rap and club music when I'm at work all the time. When I'm off, I try to relax and mellow out with slow jams," I replied. When I looked over to him, he was licking his lips and nodding his head to the music.

We pulled up to a little diner in the middle of nowhere. He opened the door to get out and waited in front of the truck while I adjusted my clothes. When we walked into the diner, all eyes were on us. There was a warm feeling when you walked in. An older lady sat us down in a booth towards the back and gave us our menus. I didn't realize I was hungry until I looked at the menu.

"Know what you want to eat?" he asked.

"Everything looks so good. I have no clue what I want to eat," I replied.

"Order whatever you want, it doesn't matter," he replied.

I had my mind on an omelet with some toast but, when I looked at the menu, I quickly changed my mind because there were so many selections. He chuckled while shaking his head and went to order damn near everything that was on the menu. The lady looked at him like he was crazy and said she would be back with our order.

"So, tell me about yourself," he said.

"Well...I'm twenty-six, no kids, no boyfriend, no drama," I stated.

"Just like that?" he asked.

"Just like that," I mimicked.

"I think there is more to you, but I'll let you tell me when you're ready," he said.

"What about you?" I questioned.

"Shit, you know the deal. You know the business I run, so I don't have to say that much. I don't have a chick, even though Ameka thinks that she is my lady. That position hasn't been filled," he announced.

"So, what is it that you're looking for in a woman?" I asked.

"Most niggas think they want a rider, you know, someone that will be down for them for whatever. That isn't something that I am looking for. I want a woman that will call me on my shit when I'm wrong but also know that there is a time and place for everything. I'm not a man that likes to repeat myself and I damn sure don't like drama or people that like to cause a scene. That's how you get caught up. When I'm handling business, I want someone to know that I'm doing just that and trust me because my word is everything. I want someone that I can continue to grow with. Someone who is about their business and has dreams other than being a boss' wife," he stated.

"Now that's deep. It's not a lot of men out here that know exactly what they want out of a woman. They choose to jump from bed to bed, hoping that they will find the right one along the process," I said.

When the waitress arrived with our order, we looked at each other and laughed because it was enough to feed ten people. He was a cool person, taking samples out of each plate and telling me to try what he thought was good. By the time I was ready to eat my food, I was full as a tick and couldn't eat another thing. I asked the waitress to wrap up my food so I could take it home because I had been picking at all the other food. He got up to use the bathroom and while he was away the bill arrived. My nosey ass just had to sneak a peek. It was almost three hundred dollars for just some breakfast.

Coming back to his seat, he opened the bill, pulled out some money, and asked was I ready to go. When we got into the car, we didn't head directly back like I expected. He detoured and we ended up at a little lake. There were people out there fishing, kids playing, and guys putting their boats in the water.

"I come out here when I want to get my mind right," he said.

I was about to say something when my phone rang, causing me to look down. It was my sister, Justice. "Shit!" I said.

"What's up?" he asked.

"I forgot that I was supposed to go see my sister when I woke up this morning," I said.

"Go ahead and call her and tell her to get ready. Your car won't be ready until later," he said.

Dialing my sister's number back, the phone didn't even ring twice before she was answered.

"Asha, where you at, sis? I have to get the hell out of here. She tripping. You hear her?" Justice asked.

In the back, I could hear Kandi going off about something, but I wasn't completely listening. I looked over to Budah and he had a pissed look on his face. He was no longer the cool person that I was chilling with for the last couple hours.

"TELL HER TO GET ALL HER SHIT TOGETHER!" he yelled.

"Justice, get all your stuff together. I will be there in a little bit," I stated.

I had given him the address to Kandi's house, and he was flying on the interstate. We had to be doing about 100 mph. We made it there in about twenty minutes. When we did, I could see my vindictive mother, Kandi, throwing Justice's stuff out of the door. Completely pissed, I jumped out before the truck came to a complete stop. I didn't think that Kandi expected to see Budah because when she turned around and saw him standing there she froze like she had seen a ghost.

"I didn't know you were bringing Budah here," she said.

"What difference does it make? You're still going to show your ass. Don't stop because he is here now. So, tell me, why are you putting Justice out?" I responded.

Snapping her head back in my direction, she immediately went into a fit. "Of course, you would bring your ass over here trying to save her ungrateful ass. The only thing I asked her for was some money that she should be giving me anyway. Since she doesn't want to give me any money, then her ass got to go!" she shouted.

"So, just like that, you're going to put her out? I knew it was a matter of time before it would happen," I stated.

"You damn right, just like that! Matter fact, take her ass on and both y'all asses never come back!" she yelled.

The entire time Budah stood right behind me, making sure that I was okay because the Lord knew I wanted to knock the living shit out of her but I decided against it. When my sister came out the house, she looked tired, defeated, and had tears streaming down her face as she bent down to grab her belongings that were tossed on the grass.

"Nawl, baby girl, leave that shit right there. I'll get you some new shit later today," Budah said to her.

Picking up the bags that my sister brought out of the house, we loaded up the truck and headed to my house. As we pulled away, my sister continued to cry in the back. I felt sorry for her because I'd had my share of run-ins with my mother but never to this point. This was a new low for her. I was thankful that I didn't have to grow up with her because I don't think I would've made it living with her.

"You going to be straight, lil momma," Budah said while looking in his rearview mirror, reassuring her.

It took us about thirty minutes before we pulled up to my

complex. Before we even came to a stop, Budah had this look on his face. "SHIT!" he said.

"What's the matter?" I asked.

"Do me a favor and go straight into the house. Do not entertain the bullshit that's about to happen, okay? I'm going to bring your sister's stuff in," he stated.

As we exited the truck, I saw what he was talking about. There stood the chick that was with him last night, talking to the complex's news reporter. There wasn't anything that she didn't have the tea on.

"Look, I've never been one to just walk away from anything but since you asked me ahead of time, as long as the bitch doesn't touch me, I'm straight," I said.

I walked around the truck and followed my sister who was ahead of me with her key.

"So this is why you aren't answering your phone or any of my texts?" she yelled.

"Ameka, go 'head on with that bullshit. You know I don't do drama," he responded calmly.

"You ain't even trying me with a bitch that got some shit. She stays in the fucking projects. The least you could do was not mess with a project rat!" she yelled, trying to make a scene.

I was cool on her ass until she said something about coming to my job to beat my ass. My sister had already made it in the house, so I didn't have to worry about her trying to jump in the drama or anything like that. Turning around and heading in her direction, I heard one of the dude's yell.

"Ah, shit, Asha about to stomp a mud hole in this chick ass!" he shouted.

"One thing about me is I do not play when it comes to my money. Now play pussy and get fucked," I said to her.

"Hoe, you not even worth my time. Keep your ass away from my nigga!" she yelled.

Before I could continue, I was swooped up and thrown over Budha's broad shoulders.

"What I told your ass?" he questioned.

"Do I look like one of your puppets or something? Put me the fuck down," I insisted.

Ignoring everything that I said, he continued to carry me into the house, taking me directly into my bedroom and placing me on my bed. Leaning against the dresser with his arms crossed, he just stared at me.

"What did I just tell you before we got out of the truck? What did I tell you when we were at the diner? What did I say about the drama and the scenes? You need to remember that when fucking with me," he stated.

"Look, I know what you said, but I will not play when it comes to my respect, my money or my sister. I will beat ass each and every time about those three things. Who said I wanted to fuck with you anyway?" I responded.

"I can tell by the way you're squeezing your legs together that a nigga turning you on. You're trying so hard to keep me from reading your body language but I noticed," he responded.

"Well you read me wrong," I lied.

"Yeah, okay. That's what your mouth says, but your body and eyes are telling me something different," he replied.

Walking out of the room, I followed him into the living room where Justice was watching tv and talking on her phone. Budah went out the door to get Justice's things I assumed.

"Comfortable much?" I said.

"Your car should be here in about an hour. When it gets here, call me and let me know. Lil momma, I'm going to come get y'all in a little while to take you to replace your stuff," he said, walking through the door.

"Okay," we both replied at the same time.

"Your spot nice for it to be in the projects," he said.

"I live here because I can afford it and still live comfortably. Just because you stay in the projects don't mean your shit has to look run down," I stated.

"Okay. Hit me when your car gets here," he said, walking back out the door.

"Girl, he is cute. Is that your new dude?" Justice asked.

"No, just a dude I met at my job. I can see that he comes with a lot of drama though, which is something that I won't ever deal with again," I replied.

My sister went into her room to unpack her things. It wasn't a lot of stuff because she had things at my house. When I applied, I made sure to request a two bedroom so she could have her own room. She spent time with me on my days off which was good because it gave her the chance to getaway from Kandi's bullshit and just relax. It took us about an hour to get everything settled the way that she wanted just as there was a knock at the door. Justice ran to the door while I went to get my phone. When I made it to the door, she was standing there like she had seen a ghost.

"Aye, ma, is Asha here?" the voice said.

"I'm Asha," I responded.

"Here's your car keys. It's out front and it has been washed and detailed," he said.

"Well, thank you," I stated.

"No worries. Anything for big brah," he said before walking off.

Closing the door, Justice was still looking crazy.

"Girl, what is the matter with you?" I asked.

"That was Kamari. I have had a crush on him since I was in the ninth grade and he was a senior in school," she said, blushing.

"Let me find out that my sister crushing on a little cutie. He does look familiar though," I said.

"Girl, he got a baby and everything. I doubt that he is checking for me," she said.

"Just because he has a baby doesn't me that he is with the chick or that he isn't checking you out," I responded.

I was looking in the fridge when my phone rung. "Hello," I said.

"I thought I told you to call me when your car got there," he said into the phone.

"Calm down, it just got here with someone I didn't know knocking at my door," I responded.

"Oh, that's baby brother. He straight," he replied.

"Oh okay," I responded.

"What y'all doing?" he asked with noise in the background.

"Looking for something to eat. I guess me and Justice about to hit the store since my car is back," I replied.

"Hold that thought. I will be there in thirty minutes. I have to take her to replace her stuff anyway so get ready," he said, hanging up the phone.

"I know he didn't just hang up on me," I said out loud while laughing.

4

KAMARI

I slid into Donte's car so he could take me back to my whip when my mind went to the expression on Justice's face. I knew who she was from when I was in school, and I also knew that she had a crush on me back then. She was just too young for me at that time. I had seen her a couple times when I went into her job at Connection, a store in the mall that I like to shop at. Every time that I would come into the store she would try to avoid me. She would do the most, switching customers with the other employees and everything.

She was beautiful when we were in school but, now, she was the baddest thing walking and she didn't have a clue. I could tell she tried to hide her body when she was at home or hanging out with her friends. I'm assuming because she was ashamed of it, but I didn't have an idea as to why. I had been checking on her every so often, and I had some of the guys around her way look out for her. They knew not to try her because I was determined to make her mine. I had gotten some background from Sham and Luck about a day ago, and they told me that her mom and pop had a problem with the nose candy. They would always trip out on her when they didn't have any money. I still needed to handle a few things but I would take care of that when I was ready to lock shorty down.

When Dontae dropped me off to my car, I decided to go over to Kendra's house. She was my baby momma but not by choice. Still to this day, I believe that she poked holes in the condoms because she knew I wasn't ready for any kids. Once Blessing was born though, I couldn't deny her. I wanted to give her the world from the moment that I saw her. Before I could make it to her house, she called me with an attitude.

"Umm, when you coming to see Blessing?" Kendra asked.

"I'm headed that way right now," I responded.

"Can you bring me some money? Blessing need some stuff," she said.

"What the fuck could she possibly need?" I questioned.

"She needs some pampers, formula, and wipes," she responded.

"You a lie. I know for a fact that my aunt stocked up on every size you could possibly need so dead that shit. I'll grab the formula and bring it over," I stated.

"I don't know why you are acting like your baby doesn't need things," she responded.

"Kendra, when you told me you were having my seed, I told you that I would make sure that my child was taken care of. Taking care of you is out of the question," I stated.

"So you don't expect me to look good too?" she asked.

"You can look however you want, but I won't be paying for it. The fuck you thought?" I responded.

Hanging up on her, I decided that I would just go ahead and handle some business so that I could chill for the rest of the day. I didn't feel like dealing with her shit today. I would go and get Blessing tomorrow and spend all day with her. I stopped by a couple of the houses to collect the money for the week so that it could be counted and deposited into the bank. We had about twenty houses scattered around the city but only a trusted few knew where they were. We had our Aunt Nairobi count our money; she was the only one that we felt we could trust. My aunt Robi took us in after our mom and dad died in a car accident when no one else in the family would.

I was about six years old and Kairo was about twelve years old. Yeah, his name is Kairo. No one calls him that unless they are family though. My Aunt Robi struggled to take care of Kairo, myself, and Miya, her four-year-old daughter at the time. She treated us all like we were her kids and didn't show favoritism, although Miya got away with everything. It was cool, though; she was the baby. Even to this day, we treated her like a baby. She was about to graduate in a couple months and Kairo had already made sure that the money for the entire four years of college was ready when it was time for her to leave.

When I pulled up to my aunt's house, Miya was sitting on the steps looking crazy.

"What's up, baby sis?" I said.

"What's up, bro?" she replied.

When she said that, I had to look at her because something was wrong. There had never been a time that I came over and she didn't ask me for some money. She had this look on her face that told me that something was going on. I knew she didn't want to tell me, but she knew that I wasn't the one she needed to be worried about; it was Kairo. That nigga didn't have it all when it came to her.

"What's the matter with you?' I asked.

"Ain't shit wrong with her. I told her ass to stop hanging around the nappy head boy Javion," my Aunt said, coming out the house.

"What she talking about?" I asked.

Javion was the brother of Kaleb, a dude that we had beef with a couple years back. For my sister to be messing with his brother, I knew that trouble was brewing, especially once Kairo found out.

"It's nothing," Miya said.

"Miya, be straight with me. You feeling the lil nigga?" I asked.

She looked down to the ground with tears in her eyes and nodded her head yes.

"You know I have to tell Kairo, right?" I stated.

Flying off the steps and into my arms crying, she begged me not to tell Kairo. "Please, no, he will kill me," she cried.

"Well your ass should've thought about that before all of this happened!" my Aunt shouted.

"We will talk to him together," I said.

Walking into the house, my aunt Already had the bags of money ready for to me take to the bank. We had an accountant on our team that gave us the ins and outs of how to make the deposits and not set off the authority. Our accountant told us to invest in a couple businesses that made good money so it would look legit when we made deposits into our personal bank accounts from these companies. We had about eight different businesses that we would make small deposits into over the next couple days so it wouldn't alert anyone.

Kissing my Aunt and Sister, I told her that I would set something up so that we could talk to Kairo about the little nigga. I also told her that if Kairo wasn't cool with the situation she better be ready to dead whatever she had going on because she knew he didn't care about killing anyone.

5

JUSTICE

We had been riding for about twenty minutes and the entire time my mind was on the fight that my mother and I had. I couldn't believe that she had put me out because I wouldn't give her any money after she didn't come get me from work. It felt like she was treating me like I wasn't her daughter but someone off the streets. Last night, I sent her a text when I was almost finished with my shift so like I did on most nights so she could come get me. She sent me a text back thirty minutes later telling me that she didn't have any gas and to find a way home.

I didn't know why she waited so long to tell me that she couldn't get me. Had she told me that sooner, I could've got off early so I could've caught the bus home. I was stuck outside with no ride because the buses stopped running. Luckily, my friend Drea and her boyfriend offered to give me a ride since they were headed that way anyway. It was minutes before midnight when I walked in the house.

As soon as I stepped inside, my mother started going in on me because of the time that I had gotten home. If she would've picked me up, I wouldn't have had that issue.

"Justice, you hear me talking to you?" Budah asked.

"Huh?" I asked.

"What you back there thinking about, girl?" Asha asked.

"Just thinking how all of this was mom's fault and she still kicked me out," I responded.

"I know, sis. It will work itself out," Asha replied.

We pulled up to the mall, and Budha's phone rung. I heard him tell someone that we were at the mall and to come through as he was walking ahead of Asha and me. We walked around the mall, going in and out of different stores. I couldn't find anything that I wanted though. I think it was because Budah was with us and he made me nervous for some reason. It wasn't until he gave Asha some money and left out one of the stores that I was able to find a couple things that I wanted.

When we finished there, we headed over to a shoe store where I got a couple pair of shoes and sandals to match my new outfits. He had given her enough money so that she was able to grab a couple things for herself too. We were walking out of the shoe store when we met up with none other than his brother, Kamari.

There he was standing there looking good as hell. I immediately noticed that he had changed his clothes from what he had on earlier. He always looked good when he was in school or when he came into my store, but it was something different about him today. I stood there looking at him, waiting to see if someone would say something. It took Asha to speak up first.

"Aren't you the one that brought my car to me?" she asked.

"Yea, that would be me. What's up, Justice?" he responded.

"Hey," I replied shyly.

As Budah and his brother began to walk ahead of Asha and me, we were stopped in our tracks when some chick walked up to Kamari yelling.

"I know you didn't neglect coming to see your child so you could come to the mall!" she yelled.

"Kendra, what the hell are you talking about?" he responded.

"Come on, brah, tame ya people," Budah said.

"Budah, don't play with me. He was supposed to come see Blessing but decided not to come so he could come hang out with this rat faced ass bitch," she said.

I turned around to see who she was calling rat face because she wasn't talking about me with her stomach hanging over her too small shorts.

"Yeah, I'm talking about you!" she yelled.

"Kendra, go 'head on with the bullshit. You know I don't do all that loud talking, and you know why I ain't come over," he said.

"Yeah, whatever. Give me some money so I can get some stuff," she said.

"What I look like, your man or something? You brought your ass here before you knew I was here so spend whatever money you were going to spend because you won't get any from me," he replied.

Stomping off with her friends, I shook my head at her. She came and showed her ass, only for her to leave embarrassed. We continued walking and eventually split into different stores. Budah and Asha were ahead of us while he and I talked.

"You graduate this year, don't you?" he asked.

"Yeah, in a couple more months," I replied.

"What's the plan afterward?" he questioned.

"I really want to go to medical school, but I don't think that will happen, especially since my parents can barely take care of me now," I stated.

"What you mean by that?" he asked.

"Come on, you know just like everyone else that my parents have a nose candy problem despite how they try to hide it," I stated.

"No judgment on my end. No one is perfect," he said.

I stopped at the jewelry store where I had been paying on a jewelry set for the longest. The owner was cool people and let me make payments on the set and put it up for me.

"Hey, Mr. Abdul," I said.

"Hello, Justice. Here to make a payment?" he asked.

"Yes, and can you tell me the balance when you're done?" I said, handing him the money.

"You have two hundred left on it," he replied.

Walking out the store with Kamari behind me, I tried to catch up with my sister and Budah, but they were too far away.

Kamari wanted to go into one of the baby stores. He said that he wanted to get his daughter a couple things, and I didn't mind because their baby stuff was always so cute.

"Would you pick out a couple outfits for my daughter?" he asked.

"Sure, what does she need?" I questioned.

"She doesn't need anything. I just want to get her some more clothes," he responded.

Going through the racks of baby things, I picked out some shirts with the little tutus and some shorts because it was hot. They had the cutest swimsuit for her that I picked out along with the robe to match. Of course, Kamari looked at me like I was crazy, but I laughed it off. When it was time to ring up the items that I picked out, it came close to eight hundred dollars. He paid for the stuff and we were on to the next store.

We were walking through the mall and I felt the stares of the chicks that were whispering. I was sure they were talking about me. I wasn't even dressed to be at the mall. I had on a pair of shorts with a tank top. Compared to what he had on, it made me look and feel like a charity case in everyone's eyes. I began to feel uncomfortable walking next to him with what I was wearing and my hair wasn't done.

"Stop looking like that," he said.

"What are you talking about?" I replied.

"I'm watching your reaction to people looking at you with me. Stop letting the looks get to you," he said.

"What do you mean?" I asked.

Stopping in the middle of the crowd, he turned to me and said, "It's clear to see that my brother is feeling your sister, so that means we will more than likely be seen together. I want you to be comfortable when people looking at you and me. It's a turn on when a woman is beautiful and confident at the same time. I know that you are beautiful, but do you know it? I already saw what you working with when you are at work. Why do you hide your shape? Is it because you're ashamed?" he questioned.

"I guess you're right. I'm kind of embarrassed," I said.

"Baby girl, there isn't any guessing. You either know or you don't. There isn't anything to be embarrassed about. No one is perfect," he responded.

We went back to walking, and I had this newfound confidence. Thanks to Kamari, I wanted to do something to my hair, put some decent clothes on, and just look cute for a change. I had a hidden talent that no one really knew about other than Asha, and that was hair and make-up. I could watch a YouTube video on a hairstyle and would be able to do it with no problem.

I knew I had to step my game up if I was going to start being around Kamari. He was right; I did have a bad ass shape. Everytime I would walk in the hood, I would get the catcalls,whistles, and the, "Aye, shawty," to the point that I just started wearing baggy clothes, hoping that they wouldn't notice me. When we got back to the house, the first thing I was going to do was call my girl Shelley who sells hair and install me some bundles to get myself together.

6

ASHA

Budah thought he was slick when we met up with his brother. When I saw him walk up and Justice started to blush, I knew that she liked him more than she had let on. We decided to give them some space so that they could get to know each other. His dumb ass baby momma almost got beat up and didn't even know it. I played about a lot of things but my sister wasn't one of them. I would lay hands on everyone about her.

We walked off once Kamari was able to cut the drama before it went too far. Hanging around Budah was something that I could get used to, but I didn't want him to think that I was talking to him because he was a boss because that wasn't the case. I just enjoyed being around him. Sure, he had given me money to spend, but I wanted him to know that I was an independent woman able to take care of herself.

We stopped at the food court and ordered our food. I whipped out my debit card before the cashier told us the total. When I did that, I looked at him and he had this impressed look on his face, like no one had ever done that before. I mean, the least I could do was pay for his meal. Even if it wasn't much, it was the thought that counted. While waiting for our food, he told me that it wasn't often that people did something so small and thanked me. I politely let him know I wasn't like everyone else so he shouldn't be surprised if it happened often.

As we were eating, Justice and Kamari found us with their food and joined us to eat. Something was going on with my sister and I couldn't wait until we got home so that she could tell me. Once we were finished, Kamari offered to give Justice a ride to the house, and Budah said that he would take me home after he made a stop. We went our separate ways with Kamari headed to the interstate. I had no clue on where we were going, but I was enjoying the ride.

We pulled into a subdivision that had a large house at the end of the road. Hitting the button, the garage opened, and we pulled in.

"Whose house is this?" I asked.

"That was a crazy question to ask since I just used the garage opener," he replied.

I entered the house through the garage door straight into the massive kitchen. It had a double oven, flat-top stove, long island made of marble, and the kitchen sink with a window that opened to the backyard that had had a pool amongst other things outside.

"Take your shoes off before you walk on the carpet," he said, handing me some white socks.

"This is a very nice home," I said.

"It's cool. I don't really stay here that much. I just come here when I need to get away and relax, you feel me?" he said.

"I completely understand. We all need a getaway every now and then," I stated.

"Are you afraid of dogs?" he asked.

"No, why?" I asked.

Opening a door that led to what I thought was a room, he yelled, "Simba, Nala!"

I could hear the feet of the dogs. When they emerged from the door, there were two tan colored pit bulls with blue eyes; they were so beautiful.

"I come out here once or twice a day to let them out the house and to feed them," he said.

Opening the sliding glass door so they could get out, I followed him out of the door. His backyard was huge, even with the large infinity pool.

"There are drinks in the fridge and liquor on the bar. Can you pour me a glass of Henny straight?" he asked.

I walked into the house and grabbed us some glasses with ice then headed to the bar. He had every type of liquor you could think of and could open his own liquor store with them just alone. Pouring him a glass of Hennessy, I made myself a bay breeze. Walking back to the backyard, I sat there and watched him throw the ball to the dogs for a little bit. Then I texted Justice, asking her had she made it to the house. She told me that she had and was on her way to Shelley's house to pick up some hair. My sister could work magic on a head. I had been encouraging her to start doing it on a regular as a little side hustle to stack some money so, hopefully, she took my advice.

"What's on your mind, shawty?" Budah asked.

"I was thinking about my sister and how I could get her to look past what she is going through. She has a whole future ahead of her," I replied.

"Why you say that?" he questioned.

"My sister and I didn't grow up in the same house. I grew up with my grandmother, Dot, while she grew up with our mother and her father. I have never met my father or even any of his family. From what Kandi said, they didn't want anything to do with me. Kandi and Jerry both had an addiction and never really cleaned up. Our mother cleaned up just enough to be a somewhat mother to Justice but, once she hit twelve, everything went downhill," I stated.

"Wow, that's deep," he replied.

"I have always been there to look out for my sister when she was younger, no matter what my mother and I went through. When it came to school clothes, shoes, class trips, and things like that, my grandmother was always there with her," I said.

"I feel you," he said. "So what is it that you want to do? I know working two jobs to make your bills isn't the life that you want," he questioned.

"I always wanted to be a pediatric nurse," I said.

"Well, why haven't you done that?" he questioned.

"Going back to school would require a lot of time and money, something that I just don't have right now," I responded.

"If you didn't work so much and had the money, would you go back?" he asked.

"In a heartbeat," I responded.

He finished with the dogs, locked the house up, and we were on our way back to the to my house. I had to admit, his house was peaceful and put me at ease without a doubt. I was kind of sad that we had to come back to the city to the noise and drama. The reality sat in when we pulled back up to my apartment and the buddies were walking around high and asking for change for their next fix.

"I'll be glad when I get the hell out of this place. It is depressing," I said out loud.

"I'll hit you up in a little," Budah said.

I leaned over and kissed his cheek. "Thank you for everything today with my sister. I really appreciated it," I said.

"It's nothing, shorty," he responded.

Stepping out of the car, I knew that he was watching me, so I made sure that I switched a little harder so he could see these hips and ass move. Walking into the house, Justice was in her room listening to music and doing her homework. She only had a couple more months to go, and I didn't want any distractions getting in her way. She had been doing well in the medical program at the school. I was surprised when she said that she wanted to become a doctor, but I would support her in any way that I could.

"Hey, sis," I said, sitting on her bed.

In the time that we were at Budha's house, she was able to install a full weave without any help, and we were only at his house for about two to three hours.

"Hey, Asha," she replied.

"So, what's up with you and Kamari?" I asked.

"What do you mean?" she said, blushing

"I knew it. You're still feeling him, talking about you used to have a crush on him," I said, jumping up.

"Okay, he is cute, and you can't say that he isn't," she responded.

"That he is," I said, giggling.

"I just feel like I'm not the type of girl that he goes for," she said.

"So what type of girl do you think he goes for?" I questioned.

"You know…cute, small shape, pretty eyes, and long hair or something like that," she said.

"Okay, let's go into my room," I said, dragging her off the bed.

Walking into my room, I made her stand in front of the mirror. "Tell me what you see?" I asked.

"I see me," she said shyly.

"What about you, Justice?" I asked.

"I don't know," she said as her voice cracked.

Walking up behind her, I wrapped my arms around her and told her what I saw.

"Well, this what I see. I see Justice with the bad ass shape, thick thighs, small waist, and perky tits. I see a beautiful mocha complexion without a blemish and memorizing hazel eyes that anyone could get lost in. We aren't going to talk about how you don't have to wear any make-up and still look better than half of these bitches walking around the city," I said.

"I feel you, Asha," she replied.

"I want you to see what I see, Justice. More than that, I want you to feel it. I know that when you were with Kandi and Jerry you didn't have what you wanted or needed because you tried your best to help. That ended when you walked out of that door so act like a teenager and blow your money that you worked hard for. I don't care. Enjoy it now because once you're grown there isn't too much blowing money," I stated.

"I understand. I'm going to finish my homework," she said, walking out of the room.

For today to be my day off, it felt like I had been working the entire day once I laid back on the bed. Not realizing that I was that tired, my eyes closed. It wasn't until my phone went off that I woke up. I had five missed calls and six text messages from Budah.

"Hello!" I said in a raspy voice.

"She finally answers the phone! A nigga could've been dead," he said.

"What's up, Budah?" I said into the phone.

"Get up and come have breakfast with me," he said.

Looking at the clock, it was four in the morning. I didn't even realize I had been sleeping that long. "It's four in the morning, Budah," I replied.

"Yeah, I know, that's why I said breakfast. I'm out front. Let's go," he said, hanging up.

I didn't know who he thought he was, but I damn sure wasn't one of his hoes that just jumped and came running because he called. Nah, playboy, you must work for me and it damn sure wouldn't be as easy as he thought. If he wanted to kick it with me, he would have to curve that chick that he was messing with because I didn't play the second string shit. That wasn't my style. I'm first or nothing at all.

Walking outside, I had on some shorts and my hair wrapped up. Hell, I wasn't going anywhere, so I looked fine compared to the chicks that lived here.

"Come on, let's ride," he said, sitting on the passenger side.

"Budah, it's four in the morning. I'm not going anywhere but back to my damn bed," I stated.

"I know what time it is. Now, come on, a nigga hungry," he replied.

"Look, I'm not one of your hoes. You can't just pop up to my house and think that I'm going to come running. Now, I'm going back into the house so that I can get some rest. I work, unlike the hoes you mess with," I replied.

"Yeah, ight," he said before pulling off.

By the time that I made it back to the house, he had sent me a text, telling me how fucked up it was that I didn't go to breakfast with him. I replied that I knew he could find him something warm and wet to slide into and turned my ringer off.

7

BUDAH

I can't front, shorty played the fuck out of me. That was the first time that a chick had done that to me in a long ass time. In fact, the last time a chick did that was when I was on the rise, slinging rocks on the corner. I was a young dude so, naturally, I cursed her ass out and kept it moving. I remember when I stepped out on the corner. My Aunt Robi did everything in her power to keep me out of these streets, but I wasn't feeling the fact that she had to struggle to take care of my brother and sister. She was a strong and proud woman, and I couldn't think of any other way to make some quick and fast money to help her out.

I didn't feel like driving all the way back to my house tonight, so I grabbed me something to eat from IHOP and went to Robi's house. I had a key, so I didn't have to wake her or my sister to let me in. They were my heart and I would kill any and everything walking about them. My Aunt had been there for my brother and me when there wasn't anyone else, so it was only right that, when I made it big, I took care of her so that she didn't have to struggle. She lived in a large six-bedroom, four-bathroom house that sat on about two acres of land.

When I was a kid, I always dreamed of driving up to a large house on a hill with nothing surrounding me but trees. I made sure that my Aunt had the exact house that I had dreamed of. We all had a room in the house, even my niece, Blessing. She had so much stuff at the house and she was only six months. Part of that was my fault though because I didn't have any kids myself.

After I showered and ate, I went to lie down. No sooner than my head hit the pillow I got a text from Ameka's ass.

Dizzy: So u really not fucking with me like that?
Me: Yep.
Dizzy: That's all u got to say after all these years?
Me: Yep, now lose my fucking number.

I knew it was harsh, but I hadn't been feeling her ass for a little minute. Ameka wasn't always like this. When I first started messing with her, she was young, humble, dumb, and naïve. Since she had been fucking with me, she done had two kids that she didn't take care of, partied more than I did and, on top of that, her attitude was fucked up. I think the fact that she was fucking with me went to her head because she thought no one would mess with her. I did spend a couple dollars on her, but it was nothing major. I bought her a couple outfits and shoes, but that was it. She wasn't the type of chick that I could bring home to my family because she didn't have anything going for herself. My aunt always told me to never bring home a chick that didn't have their life together because she would put them to shame.

When I woke up the next morning, I could hear my aunt in the kitchen fussing about something. I laid there and tried to go back to sleep until my phones rang. It was my big brother from Philly checking to see how things were going. I had met him and his brother when they were deep into the game. I was lucky enough to get a few tricks on how to make money under the radar and how to keep my army tight because they didn't play at all when it came to that. He and I talked for about thirty minutes about a couple things and we agreed that Kamari and I would pay them a visit. We usually went up there every two or three months for our meeting with all the bosses. When I finished talking to him, Asha texted me like nothing happened a few hours before.

Asha: What you doing?
Me: Chilling. Talking to my big bro and shit.
Asha: You have another brother?
Me: Naw he is my homeboy but he treats me like family.
Asha: Oh okay. Well I'm about to start getting ready for work.
Me: Oh so u work both jobs tonight?
Asha: Yes, got to make that money.
Me: Ight hit me up later then.

I was thirsty as hell, but I didn't want anything that my aunt had in the house. She was in the middle of making breakfast so I jumped into the car and drove to the store at the end of her house. You wouldn't believe that it was a store at the end of her road because there wasn't a lot of traffic in the area. I think it may have been a total of ten houses, including my aunt's. Walking out of the store, I walked pass a chick. She looked like someone I knew from somewhere but she was a buddy, so I didn't pay her any mind.

"Budah! Is that you?" she asked.

"Shana, is that you? What's up?" I asked.

Shana had always had a crush on me when we were growing up. She just wasn't my type of chick though. She was always in some shit and, with the type of life I was living, I knew I would've been dead for fucking with her. I remember when she and her friends had set this dude up to get robbed, and he ended up killing one of their girls. I had heard a while ago that she was messing with the nigga Kaleb, and he was beating her ass every chance that he got. I felt bad for her, but that wasn't my battle to fight.

"Do you have any money that I can get? I'm trying to get to the other side of town," she asked.

Digging into my pocket, I pulled out a fifty. I knew that she wasn't trying to get to the other side of town because she had the coke head shakes. I could spot it from anywhere. Plus, she had about two other chicks waiting for her.

"How do you want me to repay you?" she asked.

"Nah, Shana, you good," I responded.

Jumping into my whip, I had to shake my head because I couldn't imagine my sister out here like that. Shana came from a good family. Her mom and pops had money, so I didn't understand what happened to her.

I started my truck and called my brother to see what he was up to. "Aye, what you doing?" I asked.

"Going to pick up your niece to take her to aunt Ro," he said.

"Oh word? I'm already there I stayed the night, ill see you at Ro house then," I replied.

"Cool because I want to talk to you about something," he stated.

Pulling off, I headed back to my Aunt Ro's house. I was inches from the driveway when I received a call from one of the workers, Tyshawn. He was a young kid that I had put on a few months back.

"Yeah," I said into the Bluetooth.

"Aye, my G, the house over on E had a bunch of white girls in it," Tyshawn said.

He was talking in codes, telling me that the house had been raided. Never had any of the houses that I owned ever been raided.

"What you mean? Never mind, I will be that way in a minute," I replied.

Hanging up with him, I bussed a U-turn in the middle of the street and called my brother.

"Aye, the house over on Emerson had a bunch of white girls in it!" I yelled.

"What the fuck the white girls doing over there? Who the fuck was they over there to see?" he asked.

"I'm not sure. I'm heading that way now," I replied.

When I arrived at the trap house, there were two buddies sitting on the side of the road while Jamal was sitting on his car. He wasn't in handcuffs so that was a good thing. Now, the big question was if there was anything in the house. This wasn't a house that did any packing, cooking or anything like that. The most that should have been in that house was some weed that could be used as personal use.

Parking down the street facing the house, Tyshawn jumped in the passenger side.

"So what the lick read?" I asked.

"There really isn't shit in the house. Ya brother came through yesterday to clear out everything so the only thing in there is a couple sacks of weed. The buddies know to say that it's theirs and we got them," he said.

I was proud of the little nigga. It looked like he had things under control better than the nigga Jamal that was just sitting on the car, watching the cops tear the house up while smoking a fucking cigarette. We sat there for about ten minutes before Mari pulled up and hopped in the back seat.

"So nobody knows who tipped them motherfuckers off?" he asked.

"Nah," Tyshawn replied.

"Anybody new been coming around?" he asked.

"Not that I can remember."

"Alright, we getting cameras installed in that bitch tomorrow. When those mother fuckers leave, shut that bitch down. I got to go grab shorty," he said.

"What shorty?" I asked.

"Justice. I'm feeling lil momma and she doesn't even know it," he responded.

I knew my brother was pissed just like I was because the whole time that I had been in the game nothing like this had happened, not even when he was working out of this house. Something didn't feel right, but I couldn't put my finger on it. I sat there ten more minutes and before I pulled off. Shit, it wasn't anything that I could do just sitting there. If anyone needed something, we had another house around the corner so no money was going to be missed in that neighborhood.

I headed to my aunt's house to hang out with my niece. I hated her mother, but I loved the shit out of her. There wasn't anything in this world that she couldn't get from me. I was even having a room done up for her at my house. I let myself in the house to find my aunt had her music playing and was in the kitchen cooking with Blessing sitting in her bouncer on the counter.

"Hey, uncle baby," I said to Blessing.

She was the happiest baby that I had ever seen. She had light brown eyes like my brother and had curly hair like her dumb ass momma. I had to admit, when my brother told me Kendra was pregnant, I was pissed because he was in no way ready for a child. He tried to get her to have an abortion but when she didn't go through with it, he had no choice but to stand in the paint and be a man.

"So, when are you going to settle your ass down with a nice young lady?" she asked.

"I'm working on it, but all these chicks see is money and fame," I replied.

"The way I hear, you be with nothing but fast ass hoes. Don't bring none of them around me, I know that," she replied.

"Aunt Ro, I don't bring them hoes over because they are exactly that, hoes," I stated.

Blessing started crying, and I picked her up. She was wet so I took her in the den so that I could change her. Yeah, I knew how to change a diaper. When I took off her diaper, I noticed that she had a diaper rash.

"Aye, Aunt Ro, come here!" I yelled.

She came in the den with Kamari right behind her. "What's the matter?" she asked.

"Blessing has a diaper rash, but this shit here doesn't look normal," I said.

"What the fuck?" Aunt Ro and Kamari said at the same time.

Her whole bottom was red. The stupid broad didn't even have the sense to get some rash cream or powder.

"I'm going to kick her ass," Aunt Ro said.

We had warned Kendra time and time again that if she wasn't going to do right by Blessing, we would make sure that her ass didn't have her. I had lawyers on standby, just waiting for her to make the wrong fucking move.

"KENDRA, what the fuck is wrong with my baby? Why the fuck is her butt damn near red and raw?" my brother yelled into the phone.

"Tell her dumb ass when I see her I'm bussing her in her shit, no questions asked!" Aunt Ro said.

When my brother hung up with her, I told him to take a ride with me to the drugstore so he could cool off and not do something stupid. On the ride to the store, he was in deep thought. I wondered if it had something to do with Justice, his new lil boo.

"So, what's on your mind?" I asked.

"Miya has been talking to Javion, Kaleb's little brother," he said.

"She has been doing what?" I asked, getting pissed.

I wasn't the big brother that went around and told my sister who she could and couldn't talk to, but that nigga, Javion, there was no way in hell.

"Bro, she really likes the lil fella and I think you should hear her out. He is ole boy's brother but they have different mothers and he doesn't really talk to him from what Miya said. I had him checked out. I think he is harmless," Kamari said.

"Call her ass," I said.

"Hey, big brother," Miya said.

"Miya, you know I'm going to kick your ass, right?" I said.

"For what?" she asked

"What the fuck you doing talking to Kaleb's brother?" I asked.

"He isn't anything like his brother," she responded.

"Listen, I want you at the house in thirty minutes after you get out of school and bring the little nigga too. I know y'all get out early today," I said.

"Okay," she sadly said.

"I'm not about to scare the little nigga. I just want to clear some things with him about her so we won't have any issues later," I said to Kamari.

"Aye, what's up with you and Asha?" Kamari asked.

"Nothing. We just chilling, nothing major," I replied.

"Oh okay. You hitting the club tonight?" he asked.

"I might, I'm not sure. What are you getting into?" I asked.

"Well, after we have this talk with Miya and Javion, I'm hanging out with my baby then I have no clue. Miya said she wanted to watch her tonight," he said.

We picked up a few creams the pharmacy tech suggested at the drug store and headed back to the house. By the time we made it back to the house, Miya was there with the dude Javion. I had to admit, he looked like one of those smart kids. You know, straight A student and totally green when it came to the streets. We told Miya to go into the house while Kamari and I talked to Javion. He was looking scared, like we were going to hurt him.

"Chill out, lil homie, we aren't going to hurt you," I said.

"Yes, sir," he replied.

"Oh, I see you have manners. I like that. Look, my sister is special to us and we don't want anything to happen to her. I'm sure my sister has told you about the history that your brother and I have. I'm willing to let all that go, but we will have a problem the moment you hurt her," I stated.

"Trust me, my brother and I are two different people. My brother being in the game has nothing to do with me. I have plans of going on to school for law in the fall," he proudly said.

"Well that's good because my sister has goals too, and the last thing she needs is someone that is going to bring her down," I responded.

"Now that we have that out of the way, come on in the house, man. I know auntie cooking her ass off in here," Mari said.

When we walked into the house, Blessing was screaming at the top of her lungs. I took off upstairs to see what was wrong with her. Miya had her in the bathtub bathing her, and she wasn't feeling it at all.

"What's the matter with uncle baby?" I said, picking her up.

"Ma told me to bathe her and put her diaper rash medicine on," Miya said.

"I got her," I responded, taking her into her nursery.

I got her settled in her outfit that my aunt had picked out for her then took her back downstairs so that I could feed her and chill before I decided to leave. I hadn't heard from Asha in a minute, so I figured that she was busy at work. I decided that I wasn't going to harass her, but I was going to the club tonight and make sure that we were seated in her section. I decided that if I was going to pay someone I might as well pay her.

Mari was sitting on the phone going back and forth with Kendra about Blessing's rash, and she was acting like it wasn't a big deal. I could see that his blood was boiling because one thing that he didn't do was play about her. Our aunt called us to the table so that we could eat. Even though we were grown, we still made time to come to her house for our weekly family meals, whether it was breakfast, lunch or dinner.

The only thing that could be heard was the forks hitting against the plates because the food was that good. Mari and I took turns eating and holding Blessing. My aunt kept trying to get us to put her down, but that wasn't happening anytime soon. She was the only baby in the family so she was spoiled as hell.

Once everyone finished eating, I said my goodbyes to everyone and went to my house. I was going to take me a nap after that good ass meal then see who I could get into before I got ready to hit the club.

8

KAMARI

I was mad as hell at Kendra for how she had been doing my baby. The only thing that she had to do was stay home and make sure that she was straight. She stayed with her momma so she didn't have any bills to pay. What was the reason for her not to handle her motherly duties? When I called her and asked how long Blessing was like this, her dumb ass had the nerve to say about five or six days like it wasn't anything. I knew I should've pushed for my aunt to take the baby because she wasn't even the motherly type. Hell, if it wasn't for my family, she wouldn't have had a baby shower or nothing. But when the planning started, her and her mother wanted to be extra and invite people just to say she was having a baby by me.

I sat outside waiting for Justice to come out from work. I wondered what would've happened if I would've put the age thing aside when we were in school. Maybe I wouldn't have the baby momma from hell. I had to admit, it was funny as hell when she opened the door the other day. She still had her bonnet on her head and was talking on the phone. We had been talking on the phone and stuff since the other day when I was at the mall with her and Kairo. I was so deep in thought that I didn't even see her walk up to the car but the soft knock on the window pulled me back to reality.

"Shit, my bad. I didn't even see you," I said.

"Yeah, I can tell that you were deep in thought. What's wrong?" she asked.

"Man, my dumb ass baby momma. I got Blessing this morning and took her to my aunt's house. Kairo went to change her diaper and we saw Blessing's butt is red with raw skin from a diaper rash that looks like she had it for months. I called her retarded ass mom and she told me that she had it for couple days," I said.

"Wow, that's messed up. Where is she now?" Justice asked.

"She is at the house with my aunt, Ro, and my sister," I responded.

"You didn't have to leave her to pick me up. I could've got an Uber," she said.

"Nah, I wanted to see your pretty face. Plus, I told you that I would. I'm a man of my word," I stated.

"Okay. Can you stop somewhere so I can grab something to eat?" she asked.

"Sure. Where do you want to go?" I asked.

"We can go somewhere quick. I know you probably have stuff to do," she replied.

"Nah, I'm straight. I don't have to meet Kairo until later," I stated.

"Who is Kairo?" she questioned.

"Kairo is Budah, only family calls him that," I stated.

Pulling into my favorite restaurant, I parked the car. I wasn't in the mood for any fast food. We stepped out of the car and walked inside to Mrs. Grace's Soul Food restaurant. I had been craving some of her greens and mac and cheese. It stayed crowded, so it gave me extra time that I could spend with Justice.

We sat in the booth in the corner. While we were looking at the menu, I noticed that Justice had really stepped her game up. Her hair was just right, and she looked like she had on makeup, but she was light with it, not overdoing it like the other chicks. I hadn't noticed that I was staring at her until she said something.

"From the way you are staring, you must like what you see," she said.

"Let's be clear. I have always been checking for you, even when you were I freshman. You have always been on my radar," I responded.

"I never knew that," she said.

"You didn't know because I know how to do things and not have everyone in my business," I stated.

We each ordered our food and, when it arrived, I don't think either one of us came up for air until our plates were cleaned.

"That was really good," she said.

"I know. Ms. Grace be putting down, don't she?" I said.

"So, what are you going to do about your daughter?" she asked.

"I'm thinking about taking Kendra to court and getting custody of Blessing. She will not use my baby as a fucking pawn. She doesn't even take care of Blessing or that nasty ass house she stays in with her momma," I said.

"Well, make sure that you take the proper steps to prove that you can take care of her because they will look at all of that," she replied.

I love that she didn't turn her nose up when I said that I might get custody and that she gave me some things to think about. I knew that I would be under a microscope for a while so this would be something that I would have to talk to the family about. I did know one thing for certain, Blessing wasn't going back to Kendra's house.

My aunt had called earlier today to make an appointment with the doctor first thing in the morning, and I was going to be there. I wanted any and everything documented. When I discussed what I was going to do with the lawyer, I needed to have all the proof. As we were leaving out of the restaurant, I kind of didn't want to drop off Justice. She was so calm and relaxing to be around. I didn't have to always be thinking ahead or always on go mode. I knew that I was going to meet Kairo at the club at twelve, so I had time to drop her off and head to the house to change.

Taking her to the house, I got out of the car to walk her to the apartment. There was a lot of niggas outside and I wanted to make sure that she made it in the house. Once we made it to the door, she looked like she didn't want me to leave, but I had to head to my house so that I could shower and change. Kissing her soft lips, I had to pull back before I took it to a level I knew that she wasn't ready for. I could tell by the way that she carried herself that she hadn't been touched sexually, and I damn sure wasn't the one that needed to be taking her innocence. I was a dog ass nigga, just like my brother. Unlike him, though, I was looking for someone that could handle me on my best and worst days, someone that wouldn't bust under the pressure.

By the time that I made it to the house and showered, it was going on twelve thirty. I texted Kairo to go ahead in and I would be there in a minute. As I was looking for something to wear, Kendra's dumb ass called me, carrying on about wanting her baby back and that she was going to Robi's house to get her. She and I both knew that she didn't want that work that Robi and Miya had waiting for her. I had been holding them off from digging into her ass but, the way that I was feeling right now about Blessing, she damn sure could get it.

9

JUSTICE

That kiss from Mari sent chill down my spine. It was something that I had never felt before. I had kissed a couple boys before, but I had never felt that way when I kissed them. Even though I did have a couple boyfriends, it was only so far that I would let them go before I would pull back. I almost went all the way with the last boyfriend I had, but I found out that he was messing with another girl from another school the whole time that I was going with him. When I asked him about it, his response was that she was giving it up and I wasn't. I was crushed when he said that.

I showered and found something to snack on while I finished my homework. I had done two classes while I was at work because it was slow, so now I had to finish my Anatomy homework. I wanted to apply for UPenn, John Hopkins, and Columbia. I had high hopes that I would be going to UPenn because I loved that city and atmosphere. I knew that it would be a strain on Asha because she felt the need to take care of me. I had been working so hard on my grades so that I could get some scholarships for school so she wouldn't have to worry. My counselor had been working with me on getting grants and references from the teachers so, hopefully, I would hear something soon.

I had been so into my homework and listening to the music that when I looked up it was going on one o'clock. I looked at my phone and saw that Mari had texted me a couple times. His last text was that he would be to the house in the morning to take me to school and sweet dreams. I had always wondered what type of person Kamari was when we were in school. He looked like the type of guy that had a flock of chicks waiting for him to just call them. I was determined not to be one of them.

As I was about to turn off my light and lay down, Drea texted me, asking if it was Kamari that picked me up from work. The tint on his car was so dark it was impossible to see who was inside. If he hadn't told me what kind of car he was driving when he asked could if he give me a ride home, I wouldn't have known either. She was in complete shock that it was him that picked me up because I hadn't told anyone that he and I had been talking for the last day or so. You should've seen the mouths drop when I hopped into the car with no questions. They were used to me getting picked up by my mother, sister or me taking the bus. So, when they realized he was waiting for me, they didn't know what to think. When we stopped and grabbed something to eat, I could tell that he was mad about something because he was frowning the entire time, but I didn't want to press the issue.

I was even more shocked when he told me what was going on with his daughter. Like, what type of mother would let their baby walk around with a bad diaper rash and then act like it wasn't an issue? I mean, come on, the baby didn't ask to be here. The least she could do was make sure that she took care of her like she was supposed to. When he dropped me off, I didn't want him to leave and the kiss only made me want him to stay longer. I knew that he had things to do and I didn't want to seem too pressed, so I didn't say anything.

I was determined to take my time with him because I didn't want to get my heart broken. I also wanted him to realize that I wasn't the type of chick that he was used to. Turning off the light, I let the music play until I drifted off to sleep.

10

Asha

I know y'all think I'm crazy for curbing Budah the way that I did, but he had to learn that he has to work for me. My night at the restaurant was busy. I had about twenty-five tables and they all tipped well. Even with me giving my portion to the bartender, I still made a nice amount. When I made it to the club, it was already packed and there were double lines wrapped around the corner. I knew tonight would be a good night. As I was walking into the back, the owner told me to hurry up because I was requested in one of the VIP sections that had the bar in it. That meant that I would be working there and there only. Although it was a grand to get in there, you barely made any money because bottles were supplied. You only made money off tips from the party, and that was if they did at all. Although it had a bar, they didn't order additional drinks unless it was a huge party.

As I was walking to the section, I heard a bunch of male voices. They were throwing money off the balcony and acting like they had it. I knew that had to be a bunch of no-name niggas that was trying to prove a point. Before I walked up the stairs, I was grabbed from behind. Turning around, I stood face to face with my ex, Nasir. He and I were in a relationship for three years. In the course of our relationship, he had two kids on me, and I fought countless chicks about him.

"If you don't let me go, I know something," I said.

"Come on now, is that the way you treat your first love?" he asked.

"Let me go before I have your ass dragged out of here," I responded.

"Do we have a problem here?" the voice asked from behind me.

Turning around, there stood Kamari, Gucci down to the tee.

"Naw, brah. This you? My bad," Nasir retreated.

"Naw, this isn't me, this is my in-law. Now move the fuck around," he responded.

"In-law, huh?" I asked.

"Hell yeah, Justice going to be my lady any day now. Don't tell her I said that though," he said.

"Yeah, okay," I said.

He ran up the stairs to the VIP section that I was supposed to be working, and it all made sense to me. Budah had requested me to work their section tonight. My mood immediately changed because I knew with him around I was guaranteed to have a good night.

When I made it up the stairs, there were about twenty people in the section, male and females. Kamari had disappeared, so I went to work behind the bar and began making drinks. As usual, the chicks were loud and the niggas were cool. I never understood why these chicks always had to be old and loud for no reason. Hell, the guys just ignored their asses the entire time. When I looked up, Budah was sitting on the sofa deep in the corner with low lighting.

Walking over to him, I stood in front of him and asked him would he like anything. He sat there quietly and didn't respond to my questions. I took that as him still being salty about last night and decided to walk away. I was about five steps away from him when I heard him speak.

"Don't walk away from me," he said.

"What is it that you want, Budah? I'm not about to play these games with you," I responded.

"Man, come here," he replied.

Standing back in front of him, he reached out and touched my thighs, sending heat waves all the way up my body. I had to realize where I was because if he kept on he might have got just what he had been looking for.

"So you just gonna curve a nigga like that and keep it moving, huh?" he questioned.

"I didn't curve you. I want you to realize a couple things and, until you do, that is exactly what you will receive from me," I replied.

Looking over my shoulder, there were people standing at the bar, waiting on me to make them some drinks. Telling him I would be back, I walked back to the bar and began taking orders. As I was making them, I noticed a group of chicks making their way up the stairs. When they finally made it completely to the floor, I realized it was Ameka from the other day at the restaurant. Shaking my head because I knew that she was about to be with the shit, I had to remember that I was working. I wouldn't lose my job because of some broke ass hoe that was chasing a nigga that clearly didn't want her.

"Well, if it isn't little Miss Thang from the projects," she said.

Her friends had already hooked up with who they came to see. I turned my head to see who she was talking to again, as I did the last time, because clearly it wasn't me. I noticed that Budah was watching me with so much intensity to see how I was going to react. Little did he know, I had a trick for her ass that would shut her mouth from here on out. Pouring a drink, Louie XIII, into a snifter, I walked from around the bar and walked seductively towards Budah. All eyes were on me and I knew it. They wanted to watch a show. Well, I was about to put on a show for them.

Standing to the side of him, I handed him the glass, as he grabbed my hand and sat me on his lap. Taking the cigar out of his mouth, he kissed me in the most passionate way that a man had ever kissed me. If it wasn't for the section being filled with people, I would've bet money we would be trying to peel off our clothes.

"So you just going to sit here and disrespect me like that?" she asked.

"Girl, it's clear that he isn't rocking with you like that. Just let go, girl," her friend said.

"Tell you what. Mook, take her downstairs and don't let her come back up here, fucking up everyone's vibe," Budah said.

Whoever Mook was, he was as strong as hell because he scooped her up like a doll baby and carried her down the stairs. Getting off his lap, I walked to the bathroom that was in the section to fix my lip gloss and splash water on my face because I knew if I was light skinned I would've been red in the face.

Taking a second to gain my composure, I walked out of the bathroom. Budah was leaning against the wall waiting for me. Damn. This man was sexy as fuck and the bad part was he knew it. Walking up to me, he kissed me again. This time, pushing me against the wall that he was leaning on. He was so close to me that I could feel his manhood poking me in my stomach and, good lawd, it had me excited. Pulling away from him, I had to move fast because his lips had me flaming hot. I could only imagine what they would do if they were on my body.

"You coming home with me tonight?" he asked.

I shook my head no because I was afraid that, if I spoke, I would say yes. I proceeded to walk back to the bar. The rest of the night was a complete blur. All I could think about was his lips all over my body. When I would look up at him, he would be staring at me like he could see into my soul. I had to take a shot just so I could take the edge off. He was doing something to me, but I wouldn't let him know that.

As the club cleared, of course, I cleaned behind the bar and counted my tips and drawer for the night. It took me about an hour and a half to finish everything. I had made five hundred in tips and I got a portion of the section also. What I didn't expect when I looked at the check that he signed was another tip of a stack. As I was walking down the steps, the manager of the club told me that from here on out Budah and his crew would be my set of clients when they came into the club. He said that they had never spent that much in one night.

Changing out of my uniform, I put on a pair of PINK tights with the t-shirt to match and some slides. My feet were hurting to no end. When I walked out to the back, there was a pearl white truck parked in front of my car with the music playing. I couldn't see who was in the truck because the damn tint was so damn dark. As I got closer to my car, the door opened and Budah stepped out.

Damn, I thought he would've left by now. I even took my time, just to make sure.

"So, about that little performance that you put on earlier," he said.

"I had to prove a point and, from the looks of it, you did too," I responded.

"Can we go grab a bite to eat?" he asked.

"Yeah, I'll follow you," I responded.

"Naw, we can park your car at the house and take mine," he stated.

Jumping into his truck after I got into my car, he followed me to the house where I parked my car and waited until he pulled up.

"So, what do you want to eat?" I asked.

"You," he responded.

When he said that, it caught me off guard so much that I had to ask him again just to make sure and, without hesitating, he repeated himself. Pulling off, we headed to the nearest IHOP. I was glad because I had a taste some steak tips. When he arrived at IHOP, it was packed with all the people that had left the club. You had the drunk bitches ready to fight while the niggas were leaning against their cars, trying their best to find out which one of them was willing or eager enough to take to the motel.

When we walked into the restaurant, the hostess told us that there was about a ten-minute wait and gave us a buzzer. As we were walking back to the car, out of nowhere, I hear a female call Budha's name.

"Budah, don't act like you don't hear me!" she said.

He kept walking as if no one was calling him and climbed into the passenger side of the car. As if the chick didn't see that he was with someone, she rushed over to the car. When she finally made her way to the window and saw that I was on the inside, her faced screwed up. Then came the attitude and the sneak dissing.

"Oh, I see that you got your side piece for the night," she said.

"Mona, you know me better than that. Anyone that I allow to push my whips damn sure isn't a side piece, unlike yourself," he responded.

"What is that supposed to mean?" she asked.

"Come on, Mona, with that crazy shit. What do you want? As you can see, I'm busy," he said.

I sat there with a smirk on my face. As fine as Budah looked and, God knows he could have anyone, I was the one that he was pursuing at the moment. As she was about to speak, our buzzer went off and I rolled up the windows so that we could go in to eat. As we were walking to our seats, he was stopped a couple times to dap people. I went ahead of him and started looking at the menu by the time he made it to the table.

Sitting beside me instead of across from me, he asked, "See anything that looks good?"

"It all looks good, that's the problem," I replied.

"Well we can order a couple things," he responded.

"No, sir, we will not order the entire menu like we did at the other place. We left half of it," I stated.

"Okay, then find something to eat," he stated.

When the waitress arrived, I settled on steak tips with hash browns, and he ordered the steak and eggs. He was so busy scrolling in his phone that he didn't even see me looking at his phone with him. I felt like someone was staring at me. When I raised my head, there was the chick Mona that Budah had brushed off earlier.

'Why is ya little friend staring over here?" I asked.

"Probably because she wants to be in your shoes. As long as I have known her, I have never taken her out anywhere. She was always a fuck and get the fuck on."

"Hmmm," I responded.

"Hmm what? Listen, I'm not about to sell you no dreams of me being a one-woman man because that isn't me. I like a variety of woman, but I do see myself settling down eventually," he stated.

"Well I want you to know that I don't play second fiddle to anyone.

So, if you think that you will be in my face and then other bitches too, you might as well think twice," I replied.

I had to set the record straight again because he wasn't used to a chick like me. My pussy was pulsating like a heartbeat the entire time. I squeezed my legs together to keep from the ocean between my legs from flowing down my leg. The entire time that we were in the restaurant, my mind wondered what it would feel like to have his lips on my waxed kitty lips. He sat so close to me so that our legs were touching. To say that I was ready to crawl on top of him was an understatement. We sat and ate in silence. He finished his food before I did because I was trying to eat cute, knowing damn well that I was hungry as hell.

"I don't know what's taking you so long, knowing damn well you want to smash that food," he said.

"I'm just about full," I responded.

As the waitress walked past, he asked her for the check. Sitting it down on the table, he pulled out a stack of money and paid for our food. When it was time to go, I gave him back the keys so that he could drop me back off home. Getting into the car, he pulled out of the parking lot, but he didn't go towards my house. Instead, he went towards the interstate.

"I live the other way," I said.

"Yeah, I know where you live, but I want you to stay the night with me," he replied.

I knew I should've driven my own car because here I was being driven to his house somehow. I knew that I couldn't get away from him. I sent a text to Justice, letting her know that I was fine and she could drive the car to school if she wanted. Pulling into the driveway, he pulled in the garage and closed the door behind us. Stepping out of the car, we walked into the kitchen. Taking off my shoes, I followed him up the stairs to this massive room that had floor to ceiling windows. He walked into the closet and came back out with some basketball shorts on and no shirt. Jesus, if my mouth didn't fall open, I would be lying. His shorts hung low so that it showed the V below his six pack.

"Quit staring, baby, it isn't what you want," he said with a smirk.

"Umm, I wasn't staring. I was thinking about something," I said.

"What would that be?" he asked.

"I was thinking that I can't sleep in this and I have nothing to wear," I replied.

"Shit, you can sleep in your bra and panties or I can get you some shorts and a tee," he stated.

"I'll take the shorts and tee please," I said.

Going back into the closet, he came back with something for me to sleep in. Showing me where the bathroom in his room was, I needed to take a quick shower before I get into bed. Looking into the closet I pulled out a wash cloth and a towel and started the shower. Pulling my hair up I stepped into the warm shower and lathered with the body wash that was already there. It smelled just like Budah. The showerheads were so relaxing that I lost track of time that I had been in it. Turing off the water I dried off and changed into my sleeping clothes. When I returned, he was lying in the bed with his hands behind his head, watching TV. I crawled into bed on the other side and he pulled me close.

"No need to be nervous. I'm not going to give you this dick yet," he said.

"Who said I was nervous? Better yet, who said I wanted the dick?" I asked.

"Everything shows that you're nervous," he said.

"I'm not afraid of you," I said, lying.

"Oh, you're not, huh?" he said, pinning me down.

Shaking my head no, I was completely shocked by how quickly he had pinned me down and was on top of me. The next thing I knew, he kissed me. This time it was with more passion than at the club. His hands traveled up my shirt as he fondled my breasts. Sitting me up so that he could take it off, I wasn't against it because I wanted it more than he knew. As he sucked on my breasts, he took his time and gave each one the same amount of attention. While doing this, he took his hand and placed it inside my shorts, playing with my soaking kitty.

When he reached my shaved kitty, he felt my wetness and smirked.

"So you don't want the dick, huh?" he said.

Taking my shorts off, he spread my legs so that he was eye to eye with my kitty. He blew on my clit, and I immediately jumped. Slowly attacking my clit, you would've thought that his tongue was a vibrator as fast as it was moving. I mean, I never experienced anything like it with any of the niggas that I ever messed with. He was a beast with it and he knew it. He came up for air to see the expression on my face.

"Feels like my tongue has batteries in it. It's okay to admit it," he said.

I was shocked that this cocky ass nigga knew he was the shit when it came to his head game. I was about to cum when he pulled away. I kind of think he knew because he pulled away too quickly. Going back down, he went back to work. I tried to get away from him, only to have him lock me in place by his strong and tatted arms.

"I'm not letting up until you give me what I want, now cum," he demanded.

I was trying my damndest to get loose from him. The next thing I knew, I was being lifted by my hips as he stood in the bed and placed against the bedroom wall, holding me in my spot. Not losing his stride, he kept tonguing me down until I came harder than I ever had before. I laid there for a minute to get myself together because this wasn't the way that I wanted things to start between the two of us. Getting out of the bed so that I could go and wash off, he stopped me at the door.

"You know it's a wrap for any nigga you fucking with, right?" he stated

"Yeah, I hear you," I replied.

"You hear me, but do you feeling me?" he asked.

Not saying anything, I walked back into the bathroom to take another shower. I hated being sweaty after sex and I needed to cool down. When I was finished, I dried off and returned to the bed where he had fallen asleep. I climbed into bed and got comfortable, thinking about what I had gotten myself into. How could he say that it was a wrap for the niggas I may or may not be dealing with when he clearly had hoes on top of hoes? Finally drifting off to sleep, I let my thoughts of Budah and I fade for another day. Lord knows I needed as much rest as I could get because I had to work both jobs and had to be on my feet all evening and night.

Budah was obviously the trick that I needed to release all the tension and stress I had built up because I slept good as hell. We didn't wake up until ten the next morning. If some lady hadn't walked into the room, talking to him all loud and shit, we probably would've slept longer.

"Kairo, get your ass up! Your food is getting cold. Shit, I didn't know you have company," she said, backing out the door.

"We'll be down in a few, auntie!" he yelled. "My bad, I forget to text her I had company last night," he said.

Getting out of the bed, I went into the bathroom to relieve myself and to wash my face. "You wouldn't have an extra toothbrush, do you?" I asked.

"Yeah, look in that drawer on the other vanity," he said.

As I was brushing my teeth, he walked into the bathroom butt ass naked, relieved himself, and then stepped into the shower like it wasn't anything and we were in a relationship. I sneaked a peek at his third leg and, when I say it was a monster, honey, it was a beast. It wasn't even all the way hard. It was the most beautiful thing I had ever seen. I took my time getting dressed because I didn't want to go downstairs and have an awkward moment with the woman, I now knew to be his auntie. When he came out of the bathroom, I was dressed and fixing my hair in his mirror on the dresser.

"Why didn't you go downstairs yet?" he asked.

"I was fixing my hair. Plus, I was waiting on you," I replied.

Taking out a pair of boxers and a wife beater, he threw on some basketball shorts with his slides, and we headed downstairs.

"Auntie, where you at?" he yelled.

"Out here on the patio, Kairo," she replied.

I followed him to the patio where she was sitting smoking a cigarette and drinking her coffee. Sitting in the chair between the two of them, he poured me a glass of orange juice.

"Thank you," I said.

"Well, Kairo, are we going to introduce me to your friend or you're just going to be a rude ass?" she asked

"My bad. Asha, this is my aunt Robi. Auntie, this is Asha," he stated.

"You, my dear, must be special. He never brings anyone to this house. It's mostly motel," she stated.

"Auntie, don't start," he said.

"What? Had I known you would've been here, I would've brought you something to eat, sweetheart," she said.

"It's cool, auntie. She can have mines," he stated. "Excuse us really quick. I have to rap with my aunt really, shawty," he said.

They went into the house and were in there for about fifteen minutes before his auntie came to the patio to say her goodbyes. As she was closing the door, the dogs squeezed past her to relieve themselves. I sat there and watched them as they played amongst themselves. They came to smell me then went back to what they were doing. Budah came back out to the patio dressed and on the phone while I finished my food and soaked in the view.

"You alright?" he asked.

"Yeah, I'm straight," I responded.

"My aunt thinks you're a cutie," he said, smiling.

"Is that so, Kairo?" I said, giggling.

"You caught that, huh?" he asked.

"Yeah, I did," I replied.

"Well, only family and close friends call me that. Most people believe that my name is really Budah," he responded.

"I see," I responded.

"You about finished here? I need to make a run," he asked.

"Yeah, let me throw this stuff away and grab my purse," I said while standing.

I threw away the trash and ran upstairs to get my purse while he called the dogs to come back into the house. Exiting the house, he closed the door behind me to the garage where he had already started his Range Rover. Pulling out of the garage, we rode in silence except for the radio that was playing. I was lost in thought, thinking about what he could've thought of me after last night.

I was snapped out of my thoughts from my phone going off. It was Justice telling me that she didn't take my car to school and she had a ride home. When I looked up, we were pulling up to my complex and, of course, everyone was out. Turning the truck off and getting out, he waited for me to exit the truck. I was wondering what he was doing. As I walked to my apartment, he followed behind me. I heard whispers as we walked through the courtyard. I knew everyone was wondering what was going on, but I damn sure wasn't about to give them any information.

As soon as we walked into the apartment, Budah walked straight into my room and laid on the bed, taking off his shoes.

"Do you work today?" he asked.

"Yes, I work both jobs again tonight," I replied.

"Aight, what you about to do?" he asked.

"I'm about to go get some food to put in the house because it ain't shit in here," I responded.

"Here, take the truck and here is some cash," he said.

"Why do you feel the need to do that?" I asked.

"Do what?" he responded.

"Give me money. I have money," I replied.

"Honestly, I didn't think about it. It's just a habit, I guess," he replied.

"Well remember I'm not like everyone else. I make shit happen on my own," I stated.

"Yeah, I know but, at some point, you're going to have to let a boss be a boss," he replied.

Stepping out of my house, all eyes were on me as I walked to Budha's truck and unlocked it. I pulled off like it was nothing and headed to the supermarket to load the house with food. When it was just me, I had quick meals and shit like that. Now that Justice was staying with me, I had to make sure that there was food for both her and me. As I was shopping, I ran into the chick from last night. She was looking busted as fuck. I wasn't sure what Budah saw in her. She must've had some fire head or something because that bitch was ugly as sin in the light.

She was with her little friend, buying crab legs like they were going out of style. I walked past them just like I hadn't seen them. I heard the fried ask, "Isn't that the chick that was with Budah?" She mumbled yeah, all salty and shit. I was smiling on the inside because I had something that she wanted.

It was like they were following me or something because no sooner than I got in line they were behind with all that loud ass talking while making indirect comments, trying to push my buttons. Little did they know, I was about to shit on her ass once and for all. I was tired of these bitches that he fucked with continuously coming for me for no fucking reason. He was the one that was playing their ass to the left, not me, so they would need to take their issues up with him.

When I cashed out, I pushed my cart slowly while walking to the truck. Placing my bags into the truck, I heard the hens in the background. The girl Mona was no longer talking shit to her friend, and I wanted to laugh.

"Girl, isn't the Budha's truck? Chile, you might as well cancel Christmas for your kids because you damn sure aren't getting anywhere with him. That chick pushing his whip took your place," she said.

Laughing to myself, I jumped into the truck. When I pulled off, Budah called. "Yes?" I said into the phone.

"So, you saw the bird brain and her friend today, huh?" he asked.

"Well, dang, she didn't waste any time calling you," I said.

"Yeah, she called me with that rah-rah. I just hung up the phone on her ass. Where you at?" he asked.

"On my way there. I should be there in about fifteen minutes," I responded.

By the time that I made it back, he was waiting for me to park. As soon I got out the truck, he opened the back to grab the food and told me to go into the house. As I was walking into my house, Justice called me.

"What's up, sis?" I asked.

"I was checking to see if you got my text," she said.

"Yes, I did get it. I thought I responded."

"I was trying to figure out what was going on with your hot ass," she said, giggling.

"Where you want this stuff at?" Budah asked.

"Sit it on the kitchen floor," I stated.

"Is Budah at the house?" Justice asked.

"Yeah, girl, he is here," I replied.

"Kamari is coming to get me," she stated.

"Okay, I'll check on you before I head to work," I replied.

I went to unpack the food while Budah went back into my room. When I was finished, he had his huge ass lying across the bed sleep. I didn't want to wake him so I tiptoed around the room while getting my things together for work. Then, I went to take a shower. I had plans on taking a nap before it was time for me to go into work.

I bathed in my favorite Victoria's Secret scent, Rush. Once I finished, I stepped out of the shower and walked into my room with the towel wrapped around me, only to find that he was lying in the bed watching TV like the place belonged to him.

"Well rested?" I asked.

"Hell yeah, a nigga needed to sleep that hangover off since someone wouldn't let me sleep last night," he said.

"Hmm, I remember someone that just had to go to get something to eat then showing me what that mouth do," I responded.

Getting out of the bed, he came close to me. Removing the towel that was wrapped around me, he let it fall to the floor. Guiding me to the bed, he sat down and stood me in front of him. Straddling him, I could feel his manhood grow underneath me.

"How do you feel about last night?" he asked.

I shrugged my shoulder because, to be honest, I didn't know how to feel about it. Yet here I was, sitting here naked as the day I was born.

"Come on, speak your mind. You're too sexy not to be able to say what needs to be said," he said.

"I don't know how I should feel. I mean, it was a wonderful experience, but I just don't want to mess up what could be," I stated.

"What do you mean? Shawty, who I put my lips on, let alone dip in for a feast, is very few and far between. I don't smash every chick I talk to, but I have gotten head from them. Nothing is going to change the vibe that you and I have because I made the decision a long time ago that you were going to mine," he said.

"What you mean a long time ago?' I asked.

"From the moment that you walked into our dining area," he replied.

"Really?" I asked.

"Yeah. Now I know I ain't shit right now 'cause I don't have a record of being a faithful nigga, but let me prove to you that I can be the man that you want and need," he responded.

As much as my kitty was dripping wet and as bad as I wanted to, I refrained from having sex with him at that very moment. He and I both knew that I wanted to, but I decided that I was going to make him work for it. He said himself that he could get pussy at the drop of a hat. Let's see how long he would last and not stray.

11

BUDAH

I wasn't sure what came over me. I had never been the type of nigga that wanted to settle down with one chick but, now, here I was telling Asha this. I wasn't sure what it was about her that made me want to change my ways. I think it was because she was a strong woman that wasn't standing there with her hand out asking me for anything. She was a cool, laid back type of chick and that was something that I was beginning to like. The fact that Robi approved was the icing on the cake. Of course, she said she was a cutie. I already knew that, but she said that it was something about her spirit that felt comfortable with her. I liked that Asha was strong and everything but when she becomes my lady the first order of business was to have her stop working both of those jobs and go back to school.

When we were talking the other day and she talked about becoming a nurse, her whole face lit up. I knew that things got in the way and she had to do what she had to do to get through but, come hell or high water, she was going back to school. She said that her sister was going to school to be a doctor so that meant she had brains too. The wheel in my head had begun to turn. A nurse, a doctor, and a physical therapist all in one spot was a good look, especially if there were all black women. I wanted now more than anything to make sure that they were successful.

I was lying there watching Asha get ready for work. I had to admit, she had a body and face that would make any chick shame. I was digging her and hadn't even tapped the pussy yet.

"What are you staring at?" she asked.

"You," I replied.

"What do you have planned today?" she asked.

"I probably will go back home. I don't feel like doing anything today. Why don't you call off today and chill with me at the house by the pool?" I said.

"Calling off does not stop the bills from coming in," she stated.

"So, let me get this straight... If you didn't have to worry about whatever bill you are trying to pay, would you call out?" he asked.

"If I had the money, I damn sure will," she responded.

"Bet. Call them now. You taking the day off," I said with much authority.

Picking up her phone, she called both of her jobs and told them that she wouldn't be coming in. Once she was finished, she took off the clothes that she had on and put on some shorts and a tank top then laid in the bed with me. We laid around the house for about an hour before my phone started ringing off the hook. Tyshawn was calling to tell me that there had been some undercover cops asking about who ran the houses.

Getting out of the bed, I walked into the living room to call my contact to see where the heat was coming from. Someone had to be talking, and I wanted to know who it was. I sent Mari a text, telling him that we needed to have a meeting asap. Shit was getting out of hand, and I had to find the root of the issue. I ran a tight ship so for someone to be loose with their lips meant that they were disloyal and no longer needed in my camp. I treated everyone like family. Anyone that went against me didn't take their life serious.

Asha came out of the room, looking concerned. "Is everything okay?" she asked.

"Yeah, everything straight," I replied.

"You hungry?" she asked.

"More than you know." I licked my lips.

"I'm talking about food, little nasty," she giggled.

I wasn't sure what the vibe was between her and me, but it was so natural, especially for two people still trying to get to know each other. Before I could say anything, the door opened, and Justice walked in with Mari right behind her.

"What you doing home?" Justice asked.

"I took the day off," she responded.

"Thank God. You work too hard," Justice said.

"See, I'm not the only on that noticed," I said.

"Mari, you called everyone?" I asked.

"You work today Justice?" Asha asked.

"Nope, I'm off too," she said.

"So what's the plan for today?" Mari asked.

"Well you and I have that thing in a little bit. After that, I'm open for whatever," I stated.

"I took off today and you're going to handle whatever business you have?" Asha asked.

"This cannot wait. It will take me all of thirty minutes and then whatever you want to do is fine," I said.

"Well I need to go pick up my check," Justice said.

"Bet. Y'all go to the mall and do what y'all do. By the time y'all finish, we should be done, and we can hang out at the house by the pool," I responded.

"We are taking both cars?" Mari asked.

"Doesn't make sense. Why don't we just take yours, and Asha can take mine and meet us at the house when they are done," I replied.

"You letting someone drive your truck other than me?" Mari asked.

I gave him a look that told him to shut the hell up. Walking to the room, I grabbed my other phone and money that was on Asha's dresser. I put my shoes on, and Mari and I left headed in the direction for our emergency meeting. We had purchased an old storefront on the other side of town. We had a 'Coming Soon' sign in the window and had a business permit pulled to make it look like there was an actual business that was going to be there so no one would notice anything.

When we entered from the back parking lot, all the bosses were there. In total, there was about three hundred of us, but this meeting was strictly for the bosses of all the crews, which was about forty. I wanted them to get the message out that whoever was being loose with their lips days were numbered.

"Gentlemen, glad you could make it on such short notice," I said.

Taking a seat at the table where Mari and Tez sat, I looked at them seriously.

"We have an issue. One of the houses on the east side was raided the other day, and I sat and watched the cops go in and out of the house. Luckily, there wasn't anything in the house because the pickup had been a day early. Someone in our camp is talking and I want to know who. I got a call today that there has been an undercover cop in the same area as the raid, asking questions about who runs this and that. I say that to say this, get your houses in order. ASAP. The last thing you want me to do is to come clean up because if I do the entire house has to go," I stated.

"Over the next couple weeks, we are going to change up our routine, pickup dates, drop-off locations, shit like that. No one will know ahead of time when and where this will happen other than Tez, my brother, and me. It's time to tighten up our bootstraps. If you can't get with the program, then you need to speak now. I will not stand for any weak ass niggas in our organization that will fuck around and get all our asses locked the fuck up," Mari said.

Since Blessing was born, my brother had really matured. I was beginning to see the man that he had become. This wasn't the life that I wanted him to live, but he fought me tooth and nail to be by my side. He was a kid when he started out in the game. I didn't make it easy for him either. I made him work out of traps. I showed him that nothing was going to be given to him so if he wanted it he had to work hard for everything.

Once the meeting was over, I called Asha and her sister to see what they were up to. They were still at the mall, so we decided that we were going to head to my house and jump in the pool.

12

KAMARI

I knew Kairo was feeling Asha. He could try to hide that shit, but I saw the way that he looked at her and the way that he slobbed her down the other night at the club. That couldn't have happened with that regular bitch, Ameka. I couldn't stand her ass with a passion. I was glad that my brother finally saw the light and stopped messing with her. I liked Asha though. She looked like what my brother needed and that was someone that wouldn't take any shit from him.

As we were arriving at my brother's house, I got a call from Kendra. She must've gotten the visit from CPS. Blessing's doctor was so pissed that she went ahead and called on her own. We had built a relationship over the last couple months that Blessing was born. I was at all her appointments, no matter what. When she saw Blessing's rash, she said that there was no way that she had that rash just for a couple days. She pointed out where you could tell that it started to heal but then it got worst due to lack of treatment. She stated that it was probably the worst case of diaper rash that she had ever seen. From the looks of it, she hadn't been changed like she was supposed to. I had been over there a couple times but when I went over she had on a fresh diaper so I didn't have to change her.

The doctor also said that she was underweight for her age. Blessing was six months old and should be at least a good fifteen or twenty pounds but she was only ten. To help her gain weight, the doctor told us to start giving her cereal in her formula. She had the receptionist schedule Blessing to return the following week so she could monitor the rash and her progress. Answering the phone, the only thing I heard was yelling and screaming.

"I can't believe you called CPS on my child!" Kendra's mother said.

"Ms. Kitty, first off, I didn't call anyone. I took my baby to the doctor. Second, who the fuck do you think you are, questioning me about what I do? You need to worry about you damn daughter and her not taking care of my child," I replied.

"If my daughter loses custody of that baby, so help me, God, I will make your life a living nightmare," she replied.

"Now, Kitty, I surely hope that wasn't a threat. You of all people should know what happens when threats are made against me," I stated.

"Yeah, well, take it how you want it," she responded and hung up.

Ms. Kitty didn't know who she was fucking with. I had all her information, knew where she worked, and what kind of car she drove. The fact that her boss was my homeboy's lady was enough for me. Fucking around, her ass won't have a job just for the fucks of it.

"What was that about?" Kairo asked.

"CPS went to Kendra's house after the doctor called them on her. Fuck her. If she can't take care of my baby, then she doesn't need her," I stated.

"So what is your plan? You know if you get custody, they will be all in your business."

"I have been planning this for a minute, just for a situation like this. I had my dude Shamar put me on his payroll for his moving company when Blessing was born, so I'm two steps ahead," I responded.

"Look at you, young man, thinking ahead," he said.

"Yeah, I had to with her ghetto ratchet ass," I replied.

"Smart move, very smart," he replied.

"Don't get me wrong, I love Blessing with everything in me. I just wish she had a different mother. What did I expect though? She was a slide and there was no real relationship between us," I said.

While we were sitting by the pool, Aunt Robi came in with Miya and Blessing. I wasn't sure who told her that we were here, but I was glad to see my little sunshine.

"What y'all doing out here?" Miya asked.

"Grown man shit," Kairo said.

"Well, grown man, ma said bring y'all asses outside and get them bags," Miya replied.

"Bags of what?" I asked.

"Ma said she wanted to grill, so we came to your house," she replied.

"Why in the hell did she come over here when she has a house with a grill that works better than mine?" Kairo said.

"I don't know, bro," I said, getting up to go get the bags.

We went outside and grabbed the bags that were in the trunk. Just as we were bringing in the last bag, Asha called Kairo because she didn't remember how to get to the house. He walked off so that he could guide her in.

"Who is that he talking to?" Robi asked.

"Asha," I replied.

"Oh, I like her. She has manners and is very pretty. Looks like I know her from somewhere," Robi stated.

"Oh God, don't start that. Her and her sister are good people. I went to school with Justice, her sister," I replied.

"I didn't say anything bad, just her face looks familiar," Robi said.

Kairo came back into the kitchen where we were, telling us that they should be here any second. No sooner than he said that, the doorbell rang. Miya ran to get the door and let Asha and Justice in.

"Asha, Justice, this is my sister, Miya. Miya, this is Asha and Justice," Kairo said.

"Aunt Robi, this is Justice," I stated.

"It's nice to meet you, Justice. Asha, nice to see you again. You ladies look familiar. What is your mom and dad name?" she asked.

"Our mother's name is Kandi and my father name is Jerry," Justice said.

"Kandi? Kandi Sanders?" Robi asked.

"Yes, that is her. Do you know her?" Asha asked.

"I used to go to school with her," Robi stated.

When she said that, she had a strange look on her face. It was the first time that I had ever seen that look on her face. It was indescribable but if I had to try I would say it was a mixture of pain, sadness, and anger. I was going to have to talk to her when no one was around.

We went to go outside to sit by the pool. Kairo told the girls that they could go upstairs to change into their bathing suits. Miya had just walked out in hers and Blessing was wearing one too. My aunt had the music playing in the house while she was seasoning the food for the grill. She had the music so loud that Kairo just turned on the speakers outside that was connected to the stereo in the house.

When Justice walked out of the house in her bathing suit, I damn near burned myself with the cigar I had in my hand. She was wearing a black bathing suit that crisscrossed in the front all the way down to her belly button. It was cut out on the sides with gold chains on it with one of those coverup things. She was bad as hell, I couldn't front.

"Justice, that bathing suit is bad as fuck. Where did you get it?' Miya asked

"Thanks, I got it from G by Guess," she replied.

"Asha, I love yours too. I have to start shopping with y'all," Miya said.

I was glad that my baby sister was getting along with them because it was hard to please her and my aunt. To see that they got along was a good thing. Justice came and sat next to me while I was playing with Blessing in the pool. She was in her baby float, having a ball kicking and splashing the water.

"She is so cute. Look at her fat, juicy cheeks," Justice said.

"This is my heart right here. Looks like someone is coming into their own skin," I responded.

"Yeah, I had a bit of a reality check the other day," she replied.

I looked over in the direction of Kairo and Asha, and they were chilling like they were a couple. Asha looked like she was made to live this life with Kairo, even though she worked her ass off. If she knew like I knew, she would stick close to my brother because once he was all in it was a wrap. He was already showing the signs and he didn't even know it. He had never chilled in the projects so to see that he was there chilling in the house, walking around in his socks and a beater, let me know he was feeling her. He let her push his whip and he didn't even let my sister or aunt Robi do that. The icing on the cake was he let her know where he stayed. They made a nice couple. Not better than me and Justice but nice.

1 3

JUSTICE

Asha had to give me a pep talk just to buy this bathing suit. I wasn't as confident as she was. My sister and I have always been on the thick side, but she could compete with the best of them. There wasn't anything that she wouldn't try to wear. She didn't care about the looks that she received because she would always kill whatever she wore. I didn't feel that way. Even with me being the same size as her, I felt that she was so much prettier than me, her hair hung down her back, she had soft skin, and was a little lighter than I was.

My sister never did anything to me to make me feel the way I did. Hell, she wasn't living with our mother when I was born, she was staying with grandma. Asha had always tried to make me feel confident. She told me that I was beautiful because I damn sure didn't hear it at home or even felt it when I was there.

"Penny for your thoughts?" Kamari asked.

"I was just thinking that never in a million years would I be wearing this bathing suit in front of you," I replied.

"Why is that?" he asked.

"I don't know. I wasn't even going to buy a suit until Asha convinced me."

"Well you're here in it now. Guess I owe sis for that," he said. "Aye, auntie, what you cooking?" Kamari yelled.

"I'm about to throw some steaks on the grill in a lil. Right now, I have some kabobs with shrimp and chicken on them," she said.

"My aunt can throw down. We been trying to get her to start a catering business but she says she just wants to relax," he said.

"It smells really good," I said.

Looking over to Asha and Budah, it looked like they were in a relationship. Although my sister hadn't admitted it yet, she was feeling Budah and, from the looks of it, he was feeling her too. My sister had dealt with dope boys in her past, but they weren't as big as Budah and Kamari. They would act and talk a big game, but she and I both knew better. That was another reason she went so hard at making sure that she didn't have to depend on anyone. She knew the risk she was taking when dealing with street niggas so she didn't stop what she was doing, which was working, because they had a couple of dollars. Budah, on the other hand, screamed money. From the top of his head to the sole of his feet, you could tell that he was dripping with money.

"Justice, come here for a minute!" Asha yelled. "What's up?" she asked.

"Nothing, why you asked?" I responded.

"You staring off like you're in deep thought," Asha stated.

"Justice, what school do you go to?" Miya asked her.

"I go to Madison. I'm in the Medical Program," she replied.

"For real? I go to Carver and I'm in their medical program too," Miya said.

"Looks like you guys have something in common," Budah said, walking over to us.

The rest of the day was nothing but chilling and relaxing. We ate, did a little drinking, and played chicken in the pool. I watched Kamari with his baby, and he was so gentle with her. He put on a front sometimes but, when it came to her, he was as soft as cotton. Their aunt was nice too. She was a hell of a cook too, but she had nothing on my grandma. Some of her food did taste like hers though. When it was time for her to leave, she told me to make sure that I showed my face more often because that she liked my spirit. That made me feel good. Miya and I exchanged numbers since she said that she wanted to link up and do some studying. Although we went to different school, we still were learning the same thing. Who knows, maybe we could learn a couple things from one another.

Asha was in the house washing the little dishes that were left while I was outside cleaning up the patio. It wasn't that much to do so I didn't mind. Budah and Kamari had vanished into a secret meeting when everyone was saying good night. I still had to get to the house so that I could do my homework and study for the three exams I had in the morning.

When they finally came out of the office, they were ready to take us home. I didn't understand why both of them had to take us, but I didn't ask any questions. The ride home with Kamari was relaxing as we rode and listened to slow music. I wasn't ready to leave him because I was having such a nice time. All of that changed when we pulled up to the apartment. The first thing I saw was Asha's car trashed.

"Aye, bro, how far are you? Asha's car is fucked up bad," Kamari said.

The next thing I knew, Asha came running over to her car going off. She had worked so hard to get that car, working overtime to keep up on her payments and have it serviced. To see that someone actually trashed it pissed me off to no end. All the noise that she was making made everyone come outside to be nosey.

"Who saw what happened to shorty's car?" Budah asked the crowd.

Of course, everyone was silent and didn't know anything. It didn't make any sense. A whole damn complex, and no one knew or saw anything, so they said.

"I got five hundred for who know what happened to her car," Budah said, walking off.

When we got to the house, it was like a damn nightmare. Our door had been kicked in and everything was ruined. The TV busted, the furniture bleached, and the food was all over the floor. Asha's room was trashed and smelled of bleach. My room wasn't that bad but, still, to know someone had been into our house and violated us like that made me want to pack my shit and move.

"What the fuck is all this about? I don't bother with no one for someone to come and tear all our shit that I worked hard for," Asha said, crying.

I could tell that Budah was pissed because his eyes were a shade darker. Kamari was pacing and making calls. I wasn't sure who he was calling, but he was on the phone going off.

"I don't care what time of night it is! I need the front, side, and back cameras ASAP!" he yelled and hung up the phone.

"Justice, get whatever you can get and let's move. You staying with me tonight," Kamari said.

Walking into my room, I gathered my book bag and stuffed a couple things that I could wear in a bag. As I was getting my things together, the police came and took a report and pictures on the house.

"So, you have no idea who would want to damage your stuff in such a way?" the lady detective asked.

"No, I do not bother anyone. I work two jobs just to make sure that I have what I want and need, and someone does this," she sobbed.

"It looks like this could be a crime of passion," the male officer said.

"The fuck you mean by that?" Budah asked.

"No offense, but her car and her house are trashed in the same night. She had to piss off someone and piss them off bad," he said.

"Look, my girl doesn't fuck with no one, instead of doing your fucking job, you trying to be nosey. Now she already told you she isn't with that beefing shit," Budah said.

It was something about the way that he spoke to the officer that showed that he wasn't scared to speak his mind. Walking out the room, the officer tried to ask me questions, but Kamari cut him off before he could even start.

"Nah, brah, we aren't doing this right here," he said.

As we were leaving, I received a call from my mother that just didn't sit right with me.

"I heard someone messed up that bitch's house and car, huh?" she questioned.

"What are you talking about?" I asked.

"Yea, just like a good sister, protecting her, of course," she replied.

"Is there something that you want?" I asked.

"So now that you have nowhere to go I assume that you will be coming home," she said.

"No, you're wrong. I won't be coming back there to live with you. I have somewhere to stay," I replied.

Hanging up on her, I got into Kamari's car. I couldn't shake the feeling that I was having when I heard my mother basically gloating because we were going through something so terrible and that my sister had lost everything that she had work hard for.

"What's the matter?" Kamari asked.

"Nothing, just thinking," I replied.

Kamari lived about thirty minutes from our apartment in the downtown area. Pulling up to a high-rise building, he punched in a code to the gate and then it opened. He parked in the nearest parking space that obviously had his name on it, right next to the elevators. Popping the trunk, he grabbed my things and we made our way into the elevator. I watched as he pushed the button to the eleventh floor then swiped a keycard. We walked to the end of the hallway and he unlocked the door. When the doors opened, a beautiful view of the city through the floor to ceiling windows greeted us. The floors were hardwood and there was marble everywhere. It wasn't decorated manly but there was a lot of neutral colors that went together well.

Showing me to my room, the first thing I wanted to do was shower and hit the books like I had originally planned.

"Make yourself at home. I'm not sure how long it's going to take to get shit straight over there, but you're welcome for however long. I'll be in the office. I have some calls I need to make," Kamari said.

Walking into the bathroom, there was a Jacuzzi tub and a standup shower. Plugging my phone into the wall, I let the music play while I filled the tub with water. I was going to relax until my skin started to look like a prune.

14

ASHA

I couldn't believe that someone damaged my fucking car then came into the damn apartment and trashed it. It took everything that I had inside of me not to break down and lose my mind. Everything was ruined; clothes, shoes, furniture... They even spray painted the walls, just fucked it up to no end. The male officer didn't make anything better, but Budah nipped that shit in the bud, which I was thankful for.

Gathering what I could, I placed it into a suitcase and he wheeled my stuff to the truck. He was waiting outside for me when some guys came to the house to fix the door and the lock on the house. Saying that he would call the landlord in the morning and give her the report number, he told them he would get with them tomorrow for the keys.

We jumped into the truck and headed back to his house. I told him I needed to stop at a drugstore or something so that I could get some personal items, so he pulled up to Wal-Mart and let me out in the front of the store. I needed to get some bodywash, a toothbrush, some underwear, bras, and other things. I really didn't buy my underclothes from Wal-Mart, so I knew in the morning or sometime tomorrow, I would be hitting the mall.

As I was about to head to the checkout, Budah texted me to grab some water and some chips. Turning around, I went to grab what he asked. When I made it to the car with the cart, Budah stepped out of the car and grabbed the items that I had. Getting into the car, I was still trying to process everything that had happened back at the apartment.

"What time do you have to be at work tomorrow?" Budah asked.

"I have to be there at five," I replied.

"Ight, take one of the cars tomorrow because I have errands to make tomorrow during the day so I can't drive you," he replied.

"Okay," I said, as we pulled into the garage.

I was so tired that the only thing that I wanted to do was rest. We had a nice day today, but I went home to a complete shit show.

"You can sleep in the room with me or you can sleep in the guest room. It's up to you," Budah said.

"Ummm, put my things in the guest room for now. If I need to move it, I will," I responded.

Placing my things in the room, he left to go let the dogs out. I could hear their paws against the marble floors. I ran me a shower and was in there for what seemed forever; it had one of those shower-heads that was in the middle and looked like it was raining from the ceiling.

After I was finished my shower, I walked into the adjourning room and sat on the bed. I was sitting and thinking about my next move. Justice was to graduate in a couple of months and go off to school. No one knew that I took half the money that my grandmother left me and started a savings account for Justice so the money had just been sitting there.

I had to go over to the apartment in the morning to see what I could get out of there. Plus, it was some things that I did want, like my important papers that I had in a safe in the back of my closet. I was so tired of thinking about what all I needed to do. I wrapped my hair up, put lotion on, and laid across the bed. I was mentally and emotionally drained. I was just going to close my eyes for a couple minutes then go talk with Budah on a time limit for me to be staying with him and using his car and things.

When I woke up, the sun was shining through the curtains. I was under the covers and my phone was charging on the nightstand. The house was completely silent, not even a TV was on. As I got out of the bed to use the bathroom, I heard the alarm go off, letting me know that someone had entered the house. As I was walking into the bedroom, Budah scared the shit out of me with a hand full of food and drinks and the dogs right behind him.

"Good, you're up. Come eat with me on the balcony," he said.

"Okay, I'll be there in a sec. Let me throw on something," I replied.

When I walked out onto the balcony, I noticed how beautiful the scene was overlooking the pool and the woods behind the house. He had my container of food sitting out with something to drink as he stared at his phone with a strange look on his face.

"Do you know any of these people?" he asked, handing me the phone.

Looking at the phone, it was a picture of three men kicking in my front door and the other was of some chicks messing up my car.

"I have never seen these people before in my life. Who are they?" I asked.

"They were the ones that were hired to break into your place. I'm not sure who they are working for, but I will find out," he replied.

"I want to thank you for allowing me to stay with you in your house and driving your car. I have no clue how I'm going to find a new spot but I know that I am not going back there," I stated.

"Don't worry about all of that. We will take it day by day," he replied.

As we were talking, his phone rang. He listened intently to whoever was on the other end of the line.

"Have you told Mari this?" he questioned.

I'm assuming that they told him no because he told whoever it was that he wanted to be the one to tell him. When he hung up the phone, he sent a text and went back to eating his food like nothing was wrong. Of course, I wasn't going to ask what that was about because if it was something pertaining to me he would've told me.

When I finished eating, I carried our trays to the trash in the kitchen. I had to get moving before it was time for me to go to work.

"Budah, have you gotten the keys to the apartment?" I asked.

"Yeah, the cleaning crew should be there in about an hour. I'll follow you over there and then go do my errands," he said.

"Okay, let me go get dressed," I replied.

I wasn't about to get all dressed up to go mess up my clothes. I just threw on some tights, a tank top, and some sneakers. When I walked down the stairs, Budah was waiting on me in some baller shorts, a t-shirt, and sneakers. Gosh, he was sexy as hell and he knew it. Standing, he turned the TV off and grabbed his keys. Handing me another set of keys, we walked out the garage.

As we made our way to my apartment, I couldn't help but feel a sense of anxiousness because I wasn't sure what was going to happen or what the landlord was going to say. Budah made it to the apartment before I did, so the door was open when I arrived. I could hear the landlord's mouth before I even made it into the apartment. She and I didn't see eye to eye to begin with but, as long as she got her money on time, she shouldn't have anything to say. Half the bitches in the complex were receiving housing assistance and still were barely paying their portion of the rent anyway.

"I can't believe this!" she yelled.

"You and me both," I replied.

"So what are you going to do about this?" she asked.

"The cleaning crew coming to clean up the apartment and to repaint the walls," Budah said.

As soon as he said that, a group of people came into the apartment. The men started to move out the furniture that was ruined while the women went into the kitchen to clean. I walked into my bedroom with bags in my hand to throw away the clothes and bedding that was bleached. As I was doing that, Budah walked into the room to tell me that he had storage for me at a warehouse with instructions to let him know once we finished. He also gave me a stack of money and told me

to go get me and Justice some clothes and stuff. I knew that I wouldn't
have time to replace everything I needed so I would grab Justice from
school and let her grab what she could.

It took us about two hours to get the apartment together. There
were two trucks; one that was going to the dump and the other that
was going to the warehouse. While we were cleaning and loading up,
Kandi had the nerve to show up. In all the years that I had lived here,
she had never stepped foot in my apartment.

"So, this is the apartment that you had, huh?" she said.

"What do you want, Kandi?" I asked.

"I just came to see if my daughter was here," she replied.

"No, she isn't here. She is in school like she should be," I stated.

"I told her that I heard about what happened and asked her if she
was coming home but she said no. So, where did she stay last night
because she didn't stay with Andrea?" she responded.

"Look, don't worry about where Justice laid her head last night.
Just know that she won't be coming back to that hell hole you call
home," I responded.

"Yeah, we will see about that. Looks like all the money that my
mother left you went to waste. What a shame," she gloated.

It was the way she said it that made me get an uneasy feeling. I
mean, we didn't have the best relationship, but I didn't think that she
would damage my stuff or have someone do it.

After she left, I did a walk through to make sure there was nothing
left. Then I called Budah and let him know that we were finished. He
gave me an address to have the guys take everything and unload it. I
headed to Justice's school to pick her up so I could take her to the
mall, pick up some underclothes for myself, and make my way back to
get ready for work. Justice was surprised that I had come to school to
get her and thought I had called out, but I told her I was still going in.

As we parked in the parking lot, the mall was already crowded.
There were kids everywhere. Justice zoomed in and out of stores like
she was on a marathon. I watched her as she picked out things that
she wouldn't naturally pick out. As we were walking to the next store,
I was bumped. Saying excuse me, I kept moving.

"Don't act like you didn't see me, bitch," they said.

Looking up, I saw that it was Ameka, the pain in the ass. Smiling because I damn sure wasn't about to make a scene with her, I continued to walk.

"Sis, who was that?" Justice asked.

"Some chick that Budah was messing with," I replied.

"Oh, okay. So a nobody? Gotcha," she said.

"That was a cute little show that y'all put on the other night. I'll see what kind of show you put on when you don't have a job," Ameka said.

I had been so overwhelmed with what I had been going through for the last couple of hours and days that I didn't remember anything. It was like it was an out of body experience. The only thing I knew was I was being pulled off a bloody Ameka by Justice and security.

"I want that bitch arrested!" she yelled.

"If I go to jail, bitch, you going right with me so what's good!" I yelled back.

She had me all the way fucked up. Why did she keep coming for me the few times that she did see me about a dude? I was glad I beat her ass. Maybe she would learn to shut the fuck up for a change. As I was walking towards the exit, I saw Budah and Kamari walking into the mall looking pissed as hell.

"I tell you to come to the mall to replace y'all shit and y'all in here kicking ass and taking names," Budah said.

"I didn't do anything," Justice said quickly.

"Well, damn, J, sell me out then," I said, laughing.

"I don't see shit funny," Budah said.

"Man, look, she had that shit coming. Since the day we met, her ass been itching for that ass kicking and that was minor," I replied.

"Yeah, but what I told you? Why you couldn't be the better woman and walk away? Come on. As my soon-to-be lady, that is some shit that you have to learn, sweetheart," he said.

"Again, who said that I wanted to be your lady?" I asked.

"You're mine, whether you want to be or not. Now come on," he said before walking out the mall.

"He told your ass," Justice giggled.

As we were walking out the door, I could hear Ameka's loud ass mouth with her friends. I swear to God if she came over here, I was going to finish beating her ass. As we stood in front of his truck that I drove, Budah finished cursing my ass out when he noticed that I had a scratch on my face.

"You know you aren't working tonight with that scratch on your face, right?" he said.

"I can't keep calling out, Budah. I have to make money. You giving it to me is nice and all, but I am an independent woman," I replied.

"Man, get in the truck and follow me to the house. We will talk when we get there," he said.

He thought that I was playing about being independent, but I wasn't. I wasn't about to be one of those women that counted on their boyfriend to take care of them. Then something happens and they're stuck up Shit's Creek. Budah looked like the type that would want to take care of his lady, which I wasn't against, but I would have to have things my way. As soon as we made it in the house, we went to the patio to sit and talk. I had been wanting to talk to him about our situation and, now, our living arrangements.

"So, I want to know how long can I stay before you will be wanting me out of your house? I don't want to overstay my welcome," I asked.

"There isn't a timeframe. You're going to be my lady in the end so get really comfortable," he said with his cocky ass.

"Okay, I guess. Well, can I at least pay you rent? Or purchase food for the house?" I asked.

"Nah, sweetheart, rent isn't necessary. If you want, you can buy the food for the house since you're hell bent on doing something," he said.

"Okay. Now that we have that out of the way, I have to get ready for work," I said while standing.

"Nah, that's not going to happen. Hold on," he said, picking up the phone.

"What are you about to do?" I asked.

"What's up, Marco? This is Budah."

"Budah, my dude, you coming through tonight?" he asked.

"Nah, I'm calling to let you know that Asha will be taking a couple days off. She has some personal things going on that she has to handle," he said.

My fucking mouth fell open. The nerve of this man to call my boss and tell him that I wouldn't be in for a couple days. I didn't even know that he knew the owner of the restaurant on a personal level. I had to admit, it was sexy as fuck though. Hanging up from Marco, he dialed another number and Stephen answered the phone.

"Damn, that's my money maker, but she does need it. It's cool, tell her to rest up," Stephen said.

"Now that we have that out of the way, let's get dressed and go out to dinner," he said.

"I don't have anything to wear," I replied.

"I can have homegirl, Sade, come over and hook you up. She has the full-service thing. Hair, makeup, clothes, all in your own home," he said.

"Have you dicked her down? I don't have time for the shit," I asked.

"Nah, she has been my homie since we were in school. In fact, I'm her silent business partner," he stated.

"Oh, well, then cool. Call her up," I stated.

"Bet. Let me ask you something, what do you think about going back to school?" he asked.

"Honestly, I would love to go back, but I can't afford it," I replied.

As we were talking, all three of his phones started ringing off the hook. He answered the one that Kamari was calling first.

"What's good?" he answered on speaker.

"Shit is hot over here off Drew. Niggas said that masked men kicked in the door and blasted on Spider, Mook, and Blaze," he said.

"Man, what the fuck?" he shouted.

"Yeah, tell me about it. It's not looking too good for Blaze," he replied.

"Man, naw, not Blaze. Where they taking her?" he asked.

I was shocked when he said that Blaze was a female. You would think with a name like that it would be a male. I walked off to go because this was business related and I wasn't sure how he felt about me hearing it. I went and let the dogs out so that they could relieve themselves. If I was going to be here for a while, I might as well start helping take care of Simba and Nala. Now cleaning up behind them shit was something else.

"Why did you walk off?" he asked as he sat beside me on the patch of grass chose to watch the dogs play.

"I figured that you didn't want me listening in on your conversation, so I let the dogs out," I replied.

"Listen, if it was something that I didn't want you to hear, I would've taken the phone off speaker. Dealing with me, somethings you will be exposed to and somethings you won't," he responded.

"I can understand that," I replied.

"I'm going to head up to the hospital to check on the workers and Blaze. Sade will be here in about twenty minutes with some clothes and her crew. Enjoy yourself and get used to it. There's more to come," he said before calling the dogs in the house.

Once he left, I was alone in this big ass house by myself. I poured a drink because I was off the next few days so I might as well enjoy it.

15

BUDAH

I couldn't believe that someone had the nerve to hit my house like that. They obviously didn't know that I ran damn near everything. I was speeding to get the hospital to check on my dudes, mainly Blaze. Although she was a chick, she was harder than a lot of the niggas that were in the crew. She was a stud, but I didn't care. She had been cool with me forever and damn near like family. I walked into the emergency room and saw Blaze's mother, her wife, her father, Mari, and Tez. Walking over to Blaze's family, I talked with them for a couple minutes to see if they had heard anything from the doctors. We were talking when a doctor came from out of the back.

"The family of Brenley Wilson?" the doctor said.

"Right here," Mrs. Wilson said.

"Hello, I'm Dr. Duran. Your daughter sustained four gunshot wounds: one in her shoulder, one in her leg, and two in her chest. We were able to remove all of the bullets except one that was the nearest to her spine. As of right now, she is holding her own although she coded on the table once. We have her sedated and will watch her closely over the next few hours. We can let visitors back two at a time if you would like to see her," he replied.

Breathing a sigh of relief, the room felt a little lighter than before. I had already received word that the other guys were fine. One was shot in the arm and the other in the leg so I wasn't worried about them. Blaze was the one that took the worst of it, which wasn't something that surprised me. She was loyal with a capital L. When she was released out of this hospital, I was pulling her out of the house and giving her something else to do. As long as she had been with us, she had proved that she was worthy to sit at the table with the rest of us.

Tez, Mari, and I walked outside of the hospital to talk for a moment. I was about to leave. I was going back to the house and would come back when things quieted down.

"Mari, have you heard anything from the insider about the raid?" I asked.

"The only thing they said they received was an anonymous tip about it," he replied.

"Tell them I need them to work harder and find out who is leaking information. I know they have a C.I. I want to know who it is," I responded.

"Tez, what about the chick you were smashing in the DA office?" Mari asked.

"Oh yeah, I forgot about her. Let me go bust her down really quick and get the information I need," Tez said.

"Ight, I'm about to bounce. I told Asha I was going to take her to dinner tonight," I replied.

"Could this be the ending of your playboy era?" Tez joked.

"Man, look, shorty got my nose open and I haven't even dipped in shorty yet," I stated.

"I guess they have that power then," Mari asked.

"Nigga, you too?" Tez asked.

"Yea, she got me looking for the future," Mari said.

"Man, naw, not you too. Shit, I ain't settling down no time soon. I got too many bitches out there to settle for just one. They loving ya boy right now," he said.

I had to laugh at him because he was a complete fool. Telling them to keep me posted, I hopped into the car and made my way back to the house. Sade had told me that she made it and, so far, she liked Asha. She knew that she had to be special if I called her to hook her up from head to toe. Not that she was looking bad, but she had lost a lot in the apartment, so I wanted to do something nice for her.

While I was driving, I called Robi. I wanted to know why she looked crazy when Justice told her who her mother was. I caught the look and, if I did, I know that everyone else did too.

"Hello, Kairo," Robi said.

"What's up, Ro? What was that look for when Justice said who her and Asha's mother was?" I questioned.

"I have a past with her," she replied.

"Ro, don't play with me. What's up?" I asked.

"Kandi and I use to be really good friends growing up. All that changed once she slept with my boyfriend and got pregnant by him," she responded.

"Okay, so, let me guess, Asha is the baby. What that got to do with her though? She doesn't even rock with her mom like that," I said.

"I don't hold anything against Asha because she didn't ask to be here. I can't stand her mother though. If it wasn't for her, Aaron would still be here if you ask me. He got killed trying to make her loose ass mother happy," Ro said.

"I feel you, Ro. Do you know any of his people?" I asked.

"Yeah, I still talk to all his people, especially his mother," Ro said.

"I'm going to see how she feels about meeting her people," I responded.

"I think that would be a great idea. Let me know and I'll work out the details," she replied.

When I pulled up to the house, I could tell Sade and her crew was still here. There was a Tahoe and a couple other cars outside of the house. Walking into the house, I heard the music playing and laughing. They had turned Asha's room into a damn store with racks of clothes. They were so into what they were doing that they didn't see me standing in the room.

"Oh, shoot, Budah, you scared me," Sade said.

"Y'all straight. How is it going?" I asked.

"It's going good," Asha said.

She was standing in a sports bra and some shorts. Just staring at how fat that ass was had my man standing at attention.

"Do you need something to wear tonight too?" Sade asked.

"Yeah, what you got?" I asked.

"I got a lil of this and that," she replied.

I looked through the rack of clothes. Sade knew that I liked Gucci so, of course, she had some. Sade was a carrier of all the high-price clothing. You name it, and she had it or could get it. She had shoes and everything all in one store.

"So, how much she spending today?" Sade asked.

"Whatever she wants, she can have," I replied.

"Oh, shit, we about to break his pockets today," she laughed.

I picked out a couple outfits and told her to include them in the total. I had Beans at the door that was coming to give me a cut. I hated going to the shop so much I had a barbershop in the basement. You fuck around and be there all damn day, just to get a cut. I let him in the house, and we headed to the basement. His shop was another one of my businesses that I was a silent partner. I believed in putting on my friends and investing my money wisely.

It took him about thirty minutes to get me right. As I was letting him out, Sade's crew was bringing down some of the clothes.

"Y'all done?" I asked.

"No, she is in the shower before we start on her hair and makeup," Kasia said.

She wanted the dick, but she was an air head and I couldn't hold a full conversation with her. I took her out once to dinner and I ended it right after. Sade was mad with me, but oh well. I went up to my room to lie across the bed and watch a movie until she was done. I must've dozed off because the next thing I know Sade was standing over me telling me to get dressed. Asha was just about ready. Sade had laid out a pair of black Gucci slacks, a white Gucci shirt with black cuffs, and the shoes and belt to match. She was a stylist, so it was her job to make me and anyone she dealt with look good. I had made reservations for nine thirty and it was eight, so I had to get moving.

Once I finished showering and getting dressed, I went downstairs but Asha hadn't made it down yet. Soon after, Sade came downstairs with everyone behind her, including Asha. She had on this long black dress with a deep V in the front that hugged her hips, thighs, breasts, and ass with a long split up the middle of the dress. On her feet were a pair of spiked Christian Louboutin heels and she had the bag to match. She was wearing makeup that didn't take away from the beautiful person that she already was, and her hair was laid just right.

After letting everyone out of the house, I pulled out my new charcoal Tesla S model from under the cover for tonight. It had been a minute since I went all out for a woman. I was hoping that it paid off in the end. Not on a sexual level because that wasn't solely what I wanted from her. I wanted to see if there was more to this connection that I was feeling.

As we were pulling out for dinner, Mari called me to give me some information on what the streets were saying.

"What's up, bro?" Mari said.

"You're on speaker and Asha in the car," I replied.

"Sup, Ash?" he said.

"Hey, Mari. Where's Justice?" she asked.

"She's at the house. I'm getting us something to eat," he replied.

"Okay," she replied.

"So, anyway, the word is some nigga name Boola or something like that is claiming that he is coming for the operation and is going to take down everything and everyone in his way," Mari said

"Where is this nigga from?" I asked.

"I don't know, but I can find out," he responded.

"Yeah, do that and get with Tez. Y'all come to the house tomorrow and we can talk about this more. Right now, I have something else I have to focus on," I stated.

I was doing good until I looked over at Asha and saw she had them thick thighs showing. She had no idea that she was driving me crazy and that my man was on rock solid. It took us about thirty minutes to get to the restaurant. When we pulled up, the valet let us out and gave me the parking ticket. I had been to this restaurant more than once with the crew so when the owner would see my reservation it was nothing but first-class service.

We were seated immediately on the far right of the restaurant with my back towards the wall. I hated sitting where people could walk behind me. Asha sat there and looked at the menu while I debated if I wanted to have the restaurant cleared to lay her ass across this table and start beating that pussy up.

"What are you staring at?" Asha questioned.

"Do you want me to lie or be honest?" I asked.

"I want you to always be honest with me," she responded.

Taking a sip out my drink, I tried to see how I was going to word this without sounding like a cocky asshole. Standing up because I wanted her to understand and feel what I was saying to her, I walked around to her and whispered in her ear so only she would only be able to hear me.

"I'm thinking about how sexy you look right now and I'm trying my best not to close the fucking restaurant to bend you over this table and fuck the shit out of you," I whispered.

I could see that she wasn't expecting me to tell her what I was truly thinking, but I spoke my mind when needed. I watched as she squeezed her thighs together to keep the juices from flowing down her leg. Walking around to my chair, I looked at the menu and waited for the waitress to come take our order.

16

KAMARI

I was scrolling through my Instagram page while I was waiting for the food to get done until I noticed that the dudes in the corner were watching me. I hit up Tez and told him to slide through where I was and bring a couple shooters. You could never be too careful, especially with some fake ass kingpin trying to take me and my bro's spot. Tez walked in about five minutes after I texted him. We didn't live that far apart so he was the first person that I would always call when I was on this side of town.

We sat there for about ten more minutes before my order was called. I got up and went to pay for my food, and the dudes that were in the corner stood up to leave. Tez paid close attention to what they were doing and so did I. When I left out, instead of me getting into my whip, I jumped into Tez's truck and we pulled off. Just like the dummies they were, they pulled right out behind us. They didn't even notice that six cars pulled out behind them.

Tez bent a couple corners and led them to a dead-end street where we parked the car and waited for them. A minute later, they came pulling up. As one of the guys got out of the car, the others sat in the car not moving. I guess he called himself having his homeboy's back, but that was the wrong move. When he got close enough for me to see who it was, I didn't recognize the nigga from anywhere. He had dreads and a tattoo on the side of his neck of a spider.

"Aye, my nigga, what you following us for?" Tez asked.

"I have a message for you and your brother," he said.

"Man, fuck your message. We run this over here, so I got a message for you to relay. If you want a war, we can go to war. Y'all mother-fuckers think because y'all move some weight that you can take over. It's isn't that simple. If you try to take what's ours, be ready because we stay ready," I stated.

"Nigga, you aren't scaring shit over this way. All that rah-rah you talking, you can find someone that's scared of your soft ass. I stay strapped my nigga, what's good?" the dude asked, holding up his shirt.

Before I could respond, the other guys pulled up from all directions and had their guns out.

"So, like I was saying before, we stay ready," I replied.

"Did you really think that we didn't peep y'all in the restaurant?" Tez said.

"We can do this the hard way or we can do this the hard way, but one of y'all mother fuckers won't be leaving here," I said.

Before I could say anything, Big let off two in the nigga's head that was sitting in the car.

"What the fuck?" I yelled.

"He was pulling out his strap," Big said.

"Well, I guess he made the choice for us so let this be a warning. Y'all handle them."

When I got back into Tez's truck, I tried to call Kairo a couple times to tell him what had happened but all his phones were going to voicemail. I knew he was going out with Asha, but he never turned his phones off. Tez dropped me off back to my truck and I headed home, watching my back the entire time. I knew that the shit was about to hit the fan, especially after Kairo found out Big put two to someone's dome tonight. I could hear him now, cursing my ass out from the front to the back. One thing he didn't like was shit not being thought out and this damn sure wasn't thought out.

When I made it back to the condo, Justice was sitting on the floor with all her books everywhere. She had been working hard to keep her grades up so that she could graduate and attend school in the fall.

"I got dinner. I ran into an issue, so we might have to warm the food up," I said.

"Is everything okay?' Justice asked.

"Yeah, everything is okay for now," I replied.

"I'll be done here in about ten minutes," she said.

I went to the room to take a shower with my mind racing the entire time. I wanted to know who was this new dude that thought he could come in and take over what my brother and I had worked hard for. I snapped out of my thoughts when I heard loud voices in the living room. Grabbing the towel and wrapping it around my waist, I walked into the living room to find Kendra and her mother standing there like two fucking pit bulls.

"I know you don't have this bitch in the house with my child!" Kendra yelled.

"First off, lower your fucking voice when you talking to me. Second, this is her fucking house as well so if you can't talk to her with respect then get the fuck out. Third, there is a restraining order so you can't see Blessing, even if you wanted to," I stated.

"The hell you mean a restraining order?" her mother asked.

Walking over to the dining room table, I came back with a court order that had been placed. The judge basically put a restraining order against Kendra and gave Robi and I temporary custody of Blessing until we went back to court. Had her dizzy dumb ass decided to show up she would have known about it.

"This is bullshit! How are you going to keep me from my baby?" Kendra asked.

"I'm going to let y'all talk," Justice said before she attempted to walk off.

"Naw, you don't have to go anywhere. You can hear everything that I have to say to them," I replied.

"Really, so you're just going to put her in our business just like that?" Kendra said.

"Anything that I have to say to you, she damn sure can hear. She isn't going anywhere anytime soon," I responded.

"I can't believe you would do this to my daughter," Kitty said.

"Stop acting like your daughter is so fucking innocent. You know damn well she wasn't taking care of my child and your ass wasn't either. So, if y'all don't mind, you can get the fuck on with that shit," I said as I held the door open.

"I hope you don't think this is over. I'm going to get my nigga to fuck you up, watch," Kendra said with a mean mug.

"Tell that nigga to come see me," I replied, slamming the door behind her.

"You okay?" Justice asked.

At that very moment, I couldn't hold it any longer. I knew that she wasn't experienced when it came to sex, but the way that she handled Kendra and her mother was sexy as shit to me. Walking over to her, I removed her glasses that she was wearing and laid them on the table. Gently grabbing her face, I kissed her soft lips. At that very instant, my man became alive. I was trying my best to contain myself because of who I was with. I was in complete shock when her hands moved from around my neck to grabbing the towel that was wrapped around my waist.

I had to stop her because I wasn't sure if she knew what she was doing or if she was even ready to deal with me on that level.

"Why are you holding my hands?" she asked.

"Come on, Justice, we both know that this isn't something that you are ready for," I replied.

"Well show me then," she replied.

"Show you what?" I asked.

Without saying another word, she kissed me again. This time it was more intense and had more passion behind it. I wanted to take it there with her but I wanted the first time that she made love to be special. Walking her into my room, I laid her back onto the bed and slowly removed all her clothes. She shyly covered herself, and I had to ask her a couple times to remove her hands. I knew she was nervous about letting me see her in this light but if she wanted to be a grown woman, she couldn't be afraid to show me her true self. I turned on Pandora and, low and behold, Chris Brown's *Who's Gonna* was playing. Just what I need to get the mood right.

Pulling the towel from around my waist, I stood in front of her for a minute. I wanted her to see what she would be working with when she was ready. I decided to put on some boxers because it wasn't about me; it was about her. I wanted her to be completely comfortable with me. Crawling in between her legs, I was surprised to see that she has a clean kitty. Most chicks that had never been touched had a bush and shit everywhere, but Justice was nice and neat. She was nervous and her legs were shaking. I eased myself up to her and kissed her lips. I took my time kissing every inch or her body, playing special attention to her breasts. As I eased myself down to her kitty, I gently devoured her in my mouth. She released light moans, letting me know that I had hit her sweet spot.

It was getting good to both her and me. She kept asking me to put it in, but I knew that she wasn't ready so I made sure she got hers then I went to take a cold shower. The hell I looked like beating my meat? As bad as I wanted her, I just couldn't. When I was finished showering again, I walked out of the room to find Justice in her shower in the other room.

"You could've taken a shower with me," I said.

She didn't respond, so I knew I had messed up. I walked out into the living room so that I could warm our food up, and she came out of the room with an attitude. I wasn't about to play games with her so I was about to nip that shit in the bud right quick.

"Justice, look at me," I said, standing at the counter.

"What, Kamari?" she snapped.

"One thing you are going to do is calm that fucking attitude down. Now, I know you're upset about what just happened, but you aren't ready to deal with a nigga like me yet. This can go either two ways. You'll have a broken heart or I'll make you my wife and we ride this bitch 'til the wheels fall off," he replied.

"Yeah, okay," she snarled.

"Look, you have dreams of being a doctor. I don't want to fuck up your dreams, ya feel me? All I'm asking is for you to think about it a little while because this is a big deal and I don't want to be that dude," I proclaimed.

"I understand everything that you are saying. Thank you for considering my feeling before we took it there," she replied.

"You have no clue how bad I wanted to, but I want to make sure that you are clear in your decision," I replied, placing our food on the table.

We sat down at the table and enjoyed our food. We talked about different things and what we wanted out of life. She was telling me that she was excited and nervous to be finally graduating at the same time. We talked about her going to her prom and she said that she didn't want to go. I, on the other hand, tried to convince her that this was her last year so she might as well go out with a bang. I even told her that I would take her if she wanted to go. One we finished our food, we threw out our trash. She finished her homework and prepared for her tests the next day while I watched TV until I fell asleep.

17

_____

ASHA

Budha's ass sure knew how to make the mood tense as hell. It was bad enough that I was already horny as fuck. Then he brought his sexy ass around to me and whispered that he wanted to bend me over the table didn't make the shit any better. If there was a bucket under me, it would've been filled because I was dripping wet. The fact that I didn't have any panties on didn't make it any better. The entire dinner was filled with so much sexual tension you could cut it with a knife. My mind kept racing back to him running his tongue all over my body.

"Asha, I was talking to my aunt and she told me that she and your mother were friends at one point in time," he said.

"Oh, really? Was that before or after she became an addict?" I asked.

"From what she was telling me, it was before you were born. She says that she knows your people's family and all," he replied.

"What people? From what Kandi said, they knew about me and wanted nothing to do with me," I advised.

"I'm not sure if that is the case but, if it isn't, are you willing to meet them?" he asked.

"Sure, I would love to get to know the other side of my family. I`t's lonely not having anyone other than Justice," I agreed.

The rest of the dinner was nice. We laughed and talked about a variety of things. We were stopped a couple times from random people that wanted to speak to him in passing. Once it was time for us to leave, I felt the tension all over again. I was going back and forth with myself to make the first move because, clearly, he and I wanted it.

Lifting up so that I didn't mess up the dress, I was bare skin on the plush leather seat. Taking his free hand that he had on the shift, I placed it on my leg. Taking the signal that I gave him, he proceeded to pull my legs apart and feel on my clean shaved kitty. The ride was about twenty minutes from the house and it felt like an eternity. He sped up and we made it to the house quicker than I expected. Hitting the button to raise the garage door, we pulled in and parked. By the time that I stepped out of the car, he had already made it to the side, swooping me up in his arms and carrying me into the house.

When we made it to the bedroom, he put me on my feet long enough for my dress to be ripped off. Leaving on the heels that I had on, I was now lying on the bed with just them. Watching him remove his clothes was enough to do me in as I focused on his muscular arms and his ripped six pack. He removed his pants and boxers, and I wanted to shout to the heavens above for the beautiful, long, thick rod that was staring at me.

Climbing on top of me, he kissed me so passionately. I laid there and felt like I was melting into the mattress. He devoured my body in its entirety. Lifting from me, he leaned over and grabbed a condom. I took it from him and slid it down his shaft. He had to be every bit of eleven and a half inches. I wasn't sure if I was going to be able to take it all, but I damn sure was about to have fun seeing how much I could take.

As he eased inside of me, I felt like he was ripping me apart. It wasn't an uncomfortable pain, more so like a pleasurable pain that I could withstand. He was right when he had said that I wasn't ready because I damn sure wasn't. He had my legs in every kind of position that he could think of. Me being a big girl, you wouldn't think that I could do some of the moves but I did them. I was never big on giving head but, with him, I just had to see what it tasted like. What I didn't expect was to be flipped upside down. He became the cookie monster.

We were all over that room that night. It was like an addictive candy that you couldn't get enough of. Just when we thought that we had enough, one of us would start all over again and another round we went. We didn't stop until the sun came up and I tapped out because I was sore as all hell. I had to take my ass and sit in the Jacuzzi and relax. Muscles hurt that I didn't know existed and all. Budah, on the other hand, jumped into the shower and went to grab us something to eat. I couldn't understand where the hell he got all the energy from. The only thing I wanted to do was lie the hell down and sleep for a couple hours.

When he returned, I could tell something was bothering him because he was mumbling and slamming things down.

"Is everything okay?" I asked.

"Not really but it will be," he replied.

"Do you want to talk about it?" I asked.

"It's best that I don't tell you what's going on so if you're asked you won't be lying," he responded.

"Okay, I was thinking about going up to Galen Nursing School to look around at the school," I stated.

"Oh yeah? That sounds like a plan. Let me know the fees and everything like that so we can get you started," he stated.

"I didn't want you to pay for it," I replied.

"Asha, you're my lady so let's stop beating around the bush. My name is written all up through that kitty so let your man be the man that you know that I am," he stated.

As I was about to respond, the doorbell rang. Opening the door, there stood Kamari and some other guy.

"What's up, sis?" he said

"What's up," the guy said.

"Asha, this is the Tez. Tez, this is Asha," Budah said.

I went upstairs because I was about to get me a good nap in before I started moving around. As I was lying down I received a text from Justice, asking how my night went. I told her that everything went great and that I was going over to the school to see about some classes. She told me how Mari wanted her to go to her prom and offered to take her. I told her that would be a great idea because I didn't go to mine and I regretted not going. After I finished texting her, I dozed off to sleep, not waking up until the late afternoon with Budah spooning me.

"Why didn't you wake me up when you came to lay down?" I asked.

"You needed to rest. You had a workout last night. We have dinner with Robi tonight at her house," he replied.

"Budah, do you want kids?" I asked.

"Yeah, I plan on filling you up with kids very soon," he replied.

"What you are talking about?" I questioned.

"Did I stutter? I want four kids, two boys and two girls," he replied.

"I'm hungry as hell. I'm going to get something," I said, getting out of the bed.

"Yeah, go ahead and change the subject but don't be surprised when you're pregnant," he said.

I walked downstairs to the kitchen to find me something to eat. Budah was crazy as hell if he thought that I was popping out four kids. Two was a maybe but, four? He really bumped his head. I didn't even notice that the dogs were out of the cage until they rubbed against my leg, damn near making me drop the plate that I had. I went back upstairs with the dogs waiting at the bottom of the steps, only to find Budah lying on the bed watching TV with his phone in his hand.

"Damn, you ain't bring a nigga anything to eat?" he asked.

"Closed mouths don't get fed," I responded.

"Damn, it's like that?" he questioned, walking around the bed.

Standing in front of me, he took the plate out of my hand and sat it on the nightstand.

"What are you about to do?" I asked.

"Get me something to eat," he responded as he pushed me back onto the bed. "Lift up," he said, pulling my tights down.

He was now eye level to my kitty. He started off by kissing my inner thigh from the left side to the right then stuck his finger inside of me, fingering me for a couple seconds. He placed soft kisses on my kitty before he devoured me yet again. He continued to feast on me until I couldn't take it any longer. He led me into the shower, and he and I bathed. The shower was nice and warm. There was a bench in the shower that you could sit on and relax with the steam. As he sat on the bench, I straddled him so that I was facing him. Easing myself down on his huge rod, I took a moment to adjust to his size.

Once I was completely adjusted, I began to rock back and forth and wind my hips in a circular motion. The feeling was something that I had never felt before. I think it was the combination of me riding him as the water hit me because before I knew it I was cumming like I had never. Before I knew it, Budah had flipped me over so my hands were on the bench and my ass was tooted up. He was fucking the hell out of me like he was going away to prison. We were so wrapped up in the moment that he released inside of me. When he realized what had happened, it was too late.

"Shit, Asha, you on the pill?" he asked.

"No, Budah, I'm not," I snapped.

"No need for the fucking attitude. We can stop by the drug store on the way to Robi house," he responded.

"Let's just go ahead and get dressed so we can go," I replied.

I went into the other room so that I could find something to wear. My hair was fucked up, but I had a trick for that though. It was going to take me about twenty-five minutes to get myself together. I couldn't decide what I wanted to wear but I eventually settled for a short romper and some sandals. Lightly beating my face, I did something to my hair next. By the time that I was finished, Budah was lying on the bed watching me in the bathroom.

"Take a picture, it will last longer," I said.

"You have panties on under that?" he asked.

"Nope," I replied.

"Good, we can sneak off," he stated.

Grabbing my bag, I ignored what he just said. If he thought I was fucking him in his aunt's house, he had another thing coming.

18

KAMARI

Kairo was pissed as hell when he found out that we had a snake in the crew. Tez said that the chick only gave the initials because that was what the reports were saying. I had seen my brother mad, but not to this point. He was almost seeing red and we didn't even know who it was. I could only imagine what was going to happen when we finally found out who it was. He had this sick, twisted way of inflicting pain on others.

Once I left his house, I went and grabbed Blessing from Aunt Ro. I wanted to spend some time with her. She had the most beautiful hazel eyes. She got them from Kendra's retarded ass, but everything else was all me. When I got there, she was lying in her playpen sleeping and Aunt Ro was watching a movie.

"Mari, sit down for a minute. I want to talk to you about something," she said

"What's up?" I asked.

"What are you doing with Justice?" she asked.

I knew she was going to ask this, so I acted like I didn't know what she was talking about.

"What you talking about, Ro?" I questioned.

"Boy, don't play with me. Justice is way too young to be playing someone's mother. I can see it in her. She has goals and dealing with you may stop her from achieving those goals," she stated.

"Ro, I'm not forcing Justice to do anything that she doesn't want to do. I want her to go to school and better herself. Yeah, I know she has goals. She wants to be a doctor and, come hell or high water, she will do just that," I responded.

"Okay, I just wanted to express what I was feeling. You know I do not hold my tongue about anything," she said.

"I know, Ro, and I love you for that. You always kept it one hundred with me at all times," I responded.

Getting Blessing's car seat and bag, I got her together so we could head to my house. We still had a couple hours before coming back here for dinner. When I got back to the house, Justice was sitting on the couch surrounded by books and papers again.

"What's up, Justice? Working hard?" I questioned.

"Well, who do we have here," she said.

Sitting Blessing down, she was wide awake and looking around with her hazel eyes.

"Hey, chunky momma," Justice said, taking her out of the car seat.

I sat back and watched the two interact with each other. Justice was comfortable with Blessing and Blessing was just as comfortable with her, which was strange because most of the time she would cry when someone new would hold her. I watched as Justice took turns doing her school work and playing with Blessing. She was even feeding her while she was reading a passage in a book. I tried to take her so that she could finish her work but she slapped my hand, telling me to find something else to do.

I went into the man cave and checked some of the emails that I had yet to respond to. There was an email from my lawyer saying that the investigation on me and my family was complete, and we were good to go. I called my connection at the police station to see if there were any other sneak attacks that were about to happen. He told me that everything was quiet on their end since they didn't find anything at the house that was raided. He also told me that he was trying to figure out who was the C.I that was giving information because they knew the layout of the house and where things should've been once they entered the house.

Hanging up from him, I became pissed that I had let my guard down and allowed someone to come into our crew and snitch on us. I walked out of the man cave and went back into the living room, where Justice and Blessing were now lying down sleep on the couch. I took off her glasses and placed them on the coffee table then went into my bedroom to lie down.

When I woke up, it was about five o'clock. I couldn't believe that I had slept that long. I must've been tired as hell with all the running around and bullshit that was going on. When I finally got out of the bed, Justice was in the kitchen giving Blessing a bath. She had her clothes laid out and was just finishing up with her. I stood there and watched her for about five minutes before I said something. Watching her made me wish that Kendra was that type of mother, but I knew that she couldn't be that person that our daughter needed.

"Do you need some help?" I asked.

"No, I'm just about done here. Go ahead and take your shower. By the time you are finished, I will be done with her," she said.

Getting into the shower, I was in there for about twenty minutes. When I was finished, I walked out to Blessing lying on the bed dressed while playing with her toys as Justice stood at the foot of the bed getting dressed. I had the bathroom door open so she didn't even notice that I was watching her until she turned around.

"You like watching me, don't you?" she asked.

"Indeed, I do," I replied.

Walking over to her, I kissed her lips and lightly sucked on her neck. She let out a slight moan, and I had to stop before I took this to the same places that I had been fighting not to go to. Plus, Blessing was there. I wouldn't be comfortable. I backed up and walked into the closet to find something to wear. She was wearing a long skirt with a cami and sandals, so I decided to go with the relaxed look too, throwing on some black Jordan shorts with the shirt to match and some Retro 8s.

Loading Blessing's car seat into the car, we headed to Robi's house for dinner. As soon as we were getting out of the car, Kairo and Asha pulled in. My sister Miya came running out of the house like she hadn't seen us in forever. Sweeping Justice into the house, we followed behind her. She wanted to show Justice something that she was working on. As soon as I got Blessing out of the car seat and put her down, Asha picked her up. I swear, this baby wouldn't know what the ground felt like with everyone picking her up. Kairo and I went out on the back porch and smoked cigars as we waited for my aunt to finish cooking. When I entered the kitchen, all the ladies were in there helping and cooking. It wasn't often that we brought women home, let alone one that would help out in the kitchen with Aunt Ro because her ass was so picky.

"So, what's the deal with you and Justice?" Kairo asked.

"Damn, is that all everyone thinks about?" I snapped.

"Woah, I just asked a question. Simmer down with all that," Kairo said.

"My bad. First it was Robi, now it's you. I'm not trying to mess up her life. I know that she has goals and shit like that, so you can save that shit," I snarled.

"Well that wasn't what the fuck I was going to say. I was about to say that I think we should send them all to school but, since you're in your fucking feelings like a bitch, fuck it. I'll do it on my own," he barked.

"Oh, shit. Yeah, that is a good idea. Especially with Justice and Miya going into the medical field," I said.

"Asha is going back to school for nursing. Maybe we can hook them up with a practice once they are finished with school. That will be a good look for them all," he proclaimed.

"Y'all come and eat," Miya said, sticking her head out of the door.

We were all seated, and Asha still had Blessing, feeding her in her high chair. I could tell that Blessing had taken a liking to her too. She was making baby sounds and trying to talk to her.

"What was that, Blessing? You coming to stay with me and Uncle Kairo?" she said out loud.

I looked at Kairo because this was the first time that I had ever heard a female other than my sister and aunt call him by his actual name. I think everyone was shocked because when she looked up we all were staring at her.

"Yes, I know that I just called him by his real name," Asha said.

Kairo, on the other hand, kept eating like it wasn't a big thing, but I knew what that meant. You could kiss the baby because it was over for any other chicks. The entire time that we were at my aunt's house, it was filled with laughter and clowning around. Kairo and I clowned my sister by telling her that we were going to show up at her prom and make a scene. Our aunt threatened to beat our ass if we did.

Asha and my aunt were sitting on the couch when she began telling her how she knew her mother, her father, and his family. She told her the story of how they were dating, and he cheated on her with Kandi after she spiked his drink. She said that she didn't find out the truth until after he was killed from being at the wrong place at the wrong time.

She explained that Kandi had kept Asha from knowing her father's family and didn't tell them when she was born. All these years Asha thought that they didn't want anything to do with her when they didn't know that she existed. She informed her that she had contacted some of the family members and told them about her, and they were anxious to meet her when she was ready.

I found it cool that my aunt had done that for Asha because everyone deserved to know about where they came from. When Justice and I decided to leave, we started to get Blessing's things together, but Kairo told us that they were taking her with them. I was going to take advantage of this free night with Justice since I wasn't going out to handle anything. I wanted to do something special for Justice for how she had taken care of Blessing today while I was off sleeping and shit. She had developed a relationship with her, and I was thankful because I couldn't fuck with anyone who couldn't deal with my daughter. She would be here forever, and I wasn't going to be like those other ain't shit niggas out here.

19

ASHA

I was shocked when Mari said that he was cool with me bringing Blessing home. She was a complete doll baby with her fat cheeks, big beautiful hazel eyes, and curly hair. On the ride home, she had fallen asleep. I had made sure that she was good and full while we were at dinner. Taking her into the nursery that was made up for her, I went into the adjoining bathroom and got a warm soap rag then took off all her clothes. Wiping her down and changing her diaper, I made sure that I put her diaper cream on thick. I put her on some pajamas, placed a blanket on her, and turned her monitor on.

I knew that I wasn't going to get my sleep like most of the time when I had a baby in the house. I had to walk and make sure that they were breathing and all kinds of crazy shit. I had watched babies a couple times before. When I walked into the room, Kairo was on the balcony smoking one of his cigars with no shirt on. Although he was sexy as hell, my body was tired and I wasn't about to fool with him tonight. Going into the bathroom, I turned on the Jacuzzi and let Pandora play on the speaker in the bathroom. Once I stripped out of all my clothes, I sat back and let the jets massage my aching muscles, thanks to Kairo. The next thing I knew, he was sitting on the edge of the Jacuzzi handing me a drink.

"Thank you," I said.

"What's on your mind?" he asked.

"Really thinking about work and school, wondering how I'm going to do all of this with two jobs," she said.

"So, quit both your jobs. I got you. All I want is for you to go to school," he stated.

"I can't have you taking care of me like that," I responded.

"Well, work one job and stack your checks then," he said.

"Okay. You're hell bent on me not paying any bills around here," I said.

"Yep, tomorrow we can go see about getting you a new whip too. No, you will not be driving that car any longer. I'm fixing it up though so you can sell it or give it to Justice," he said.

I guess he called himself putting his foot down with me and I had to admit that I was liking it. Nodding my head because I wasn't about to go back and forth with him, I sipped on my drink and continued to relax in the Jacuzzi. I heard the baby cry through the monitor and I was about to get up, but he told me to relax because he had her. When he came back into the bathroom, she was just smiling at him. It was surprising that in the street everyone thought that he was this always hard individual but, around his loved one, he was so relaxed and goofy at times.

While he took Blessing and laid her in the bed with him, I continued to relax in the Jacuzzi. When I finally decided to get out, both were knocked out in the bed. Good thing that the bed was a California king bed or else I wouldn't feel comfortable sleeping with her in the bed. Walking into the nursery to grab her blanket, I noticed she was awake by the time I made it back to the room. This time she was just lying, there playing with her feet and looking at the ceiling. Lying next to her, I watched her play silently until she drifted back to sleep and so did I.

The next morning when I woke up, Blessing nor Kairo was in the bed. I searched over the house and couldn't find them. I was about to call him when they walked into the house carrying a couple bags of food.

"I would've watched her while you went and got food," I said.

"Nah, you were sleeping well. Plus, she was up chilling," he responded.

Taking her carrier from him, I took her out and held her in my arms. I couldn't believe that he took her out of the house in her pajamas.

"Kairo, why didn't you put some clothes on her?" I asked.

"Shit, wasn't nobody paying attention to her. They were too busy looking at me with a baby, like that shit was impossible," he laughed.

"Okay, whatever," I replied.

"So, what time are you going to the school? I figured we can go look at cars later," he asked.

"I'm going to head there about ten," I replied.

"Okay, cool," he responded.

"Oh, I planned to go to the mall once I finished the tour. We can check out cars afterwards. Y'all going?" I asked.

"Yeah, we all can go. I can get Blessing some shit while I'm there," he responded.

I HAD BLESSING LYING ON THE FLOOR, AS WE WERE SITTING IN THE living room watching tv and eating. She was six months, but she was strong and trying to crawl. Kairo went to go let the dogs out. When they came into the living room, I was about to pick up Blessing but he stopped me.

"Nah, leave her right there. They been around her before," he said.

When they came to her, she just laid there and allowed them to sniff and lick her. Soon she let out giggles and started blowing spit bubbles. I sat and watched her play with them for about ten minutes until Kairo called for them to go out the door and all his phones started ringing.

"What's up?" he said into the phone. "What's up, Blaze? Yeah, come through," he said.

"Well let me get up and go upstairs and put some clothes on," I said.

"Yeah, do that. I don't want to have to go upside Blaze's head for looking at my girl," he jokingly said.

When the doorbell rang, I was coming down the stairs. When I answered the door, imagine my surprise when I realized Blaze was a chick I went to school with. We weren't close or anything like that, just had a couple classes together. Shutting the door behind her, I went into the living room and grabbed Blessing so that I could get her dressed for the day. Once Kairo was done talking, I was going to head to the school so that I could look around and see what I had to do to get started.

I bathed Blessing and put her clothes on then brushed her hair. As I was brushing her hair, she fell asleep. I put her in her crib and went to watch tv in the living room. Once the meeting was over, it looked like he was aggravated again. I was starting to wonder just what in the hell people were saying to him because every time he came out of that office he was in a bad damn mood.

"Where is Blessing?" he asked.

"She is asleep in the crib. I bathed her and put her clothes on. I'm about to head up to the school to look around. Are y'all going to meet me at the mall when I'm done?" I asked.

"Yeah, we can do that instead of you coming all the way back here," he said, walking over to kiss me.

Grabbing the keys to his truck, I headed to the garage. I backed out of the garage with him watching me the entire time. It was about a thirty-minute ride to the school, so I connected my phone to the Bluetooth and headed that way. As I was pulling up to the school, I noticed another chick that I went to school with Monica. She and I were tight in school but we lost contact when we graduated. The last I had heard, she moved to Cali for school.

"Monica, is that you, girl?" I asked.

"Asha? Oh, my God, girl!" she yelled.

"Where have you been? Last I heard, you were in Cali," I said, hugging her.

"I was, girl, but my mom got sick with cancer so I came back to take care of her," I replied.

"Oh, gosh, how is she doing?" I asked.

"She has her good days and her bad days, but she is hanging in there. What you doing here, signing up for school too?" she asked.

"Yeah, girl, I have been out long enough, and my dude is paying for it," I replied.

"Well, go ahead on then. I'm going to sign up too," she responded.

"Well, let's go ahead in here and see about these classes then," she said, grabbing my arm.

You couldn't tell me and Monica anything when we were in school. We were like two peas in a pod, and I was glad that we reconnected. As we sat and waited for the counselor to come out and give us information and take us on the tour, we caught up with one another. I told her about the Kandi situation and what happened with her and Justice, my grandmother passing, and how she treated me afterward. When the counselor came out, she took both of us at the same time. We were taking turns asking the counselor questions and even waited for each other while we were in with the financial aid office.

When we were done, we agreed that we head to lunch and chat for a while so we headed to Applebee's to get something quick to eat. I texted Kairo and let him know that I would text him when I was on my way to the mall. While we ate, she told me that she had a three-year-old daughter whose father was killed out in Cali right before she left to come and take care of her mother.

She had been looking for steady work but hadn't run across anything that could take care of her bills and be flexible with her schedule. I told her that I would check with my bosses and see if I could get her in. I had given her the short version of what had happened with my apartment break-in and destroying of my things. I knew that I had to go over there to check my mail but I really didn't want to. She agreed to follow me to the apartment since she had to go that way to get her daughter so it wasn't out of her way.

Leaving out of the restaurant, we made our way over to my apartment so I could check the mail. Kairo had called me to tell me that my car had been picked up so it could be fixed up. When we made it there, everyone was out as usual, so it didn't faze me to walk past them. We walked into the apartment and you couldn't tell that it had been broken into. The walls were painted and the cabinets and windows were fixed.

"Girl, you said they messed up your place?" Monica asked.

"Yeah, girl," I responded.

"Well you could've fooled me," she replied.

Locking the apartment back up, we walked to the mailbox to see if there was anything there but it was empty. As I was locking the mailbox, I heard the loud mouth of the apartment laughing and talking to someone. When I turned around, Ameka and two of her friends were walking my way. I shook my head because she just didn't give up. I mean, Kairo didn't want her, yet she still found the time to come and fuck with me because of it. When I finally looked at the other face, it was the chick from the night at the IHOP and the grocery store.

"Well, what do we have here?" she asked.

"Come on, Monica. I have no time for this shit," I said, walking away.

"That's right, go ahead and call Budah so he can fight your battle," Ameka said.

Turning around, I walked back to her and stood in front of her. "First off, I never need anyone to fight my battles. Two, instead of me, you need to worry about your homegirl and why she was fucking him behind your back," I replied.

"Man, fuck all that. We fighting or what?" Monica asked.

"Who the fuck is this? Your bodyguard or something?" Mona asked.

"No, I'm the bitch that will fuck your ass up. Now try me," Monica replied.

The next thing I knew, someone hit me from behind and it went from there. I had my hand wrapped around Ameka's ponytail and was fucking her ass up. I must've been getting the best of her because there was another hit. This time it was to my head. Falling to the ground, I hit my head. There was a familiar male voice when I looked up, and it was Tez and some other dude pulling Ameka off me before I blacked out.

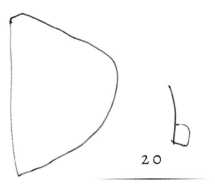

20

JUSTICE

I was enjoying the quietness of the condo while watching reruns of Being Mary Jane. Mari had gone down to the gym to work out so I had the entire couch to myself. I was in the home stretch and was more than ready to finish high school and get the hell out of here. I was still waiting on my acceptance letters from the schools that I applied to. My counselors just knew that I was a shoe in because of my grades and citizenship in the community. I was proud of my sister and her decision on going back to school. She had wanted to go back for a long time and now she was finally doing it. Taking a binge break on Mary Jane, I went down to the gym to check on Mari and see if he wanted anything to eat.

When I got down there, he was in a zone with his headphones in and sweat everywhere. He saw that I was walking up to him so he turned around to see what I had come down for.

"I was coming to see if you wanted food. I'm going to get me something to eat," I said.

"Yeah, just get me whatever you get. I'm cool with that. It's money on the dresser," he replied.

"Okay, I'll be back in a little bit," I said, leaning in for a quick peck on the lips.

When I made it back to the condo, I put on some clothes and combed my hair down then went to get us something to eat. When I made it to the diner, which was a madhouse, I ordered our food and sat outside. I figured that I would call Andrea and see what she was up to.

"What's up, girl?" I said.

"Hey, J, what's new?" she asked.

"Nothing much, just getting me and Kamari something to eat. What are you doing?"

"Waiting on Jaylin to come take me to work," she responded.

"What time you get off today?" I asked.

"I get off at five. You coming over?" she asked.

"I'm not sure yet, but I'll let you know," I replied.

"Alright, let me know," she responded.

Hanging up with her, I went back in and our order was ready. When I returned to the house, Kamari was on the phone with some-one. The only thing I heard was yelling and cursing about something. Putting the food down, I walked to the office where he was sitting behind his desk.

"Yeah, she just got here... Alright, I'll meet you there," he said.

Hanging up the phone, he stood and walked over to me. The look on his face was different from any of the other faces that I had seen. I saw the stressed, pissed, happy and goofy face, but this was one that I couldn't place.

"Justice, sit down for a minute," he said.

After taking a seat in the leather office chair, he let me know that he got a call about Asha. Other than she was in the hospital, I didn't hear the rest because I went completely blank. Jumping out of my seat, I went into the room with Kamari out on my trail. Changing out of my tights and tee, I put on some sweats, sneakers, and tied up my hair.

"Justice, what the hell are you doing?" he asked.

"I'm going to where my sister is. Where is she?" I asked.

"First, calm down. Then we can go see about your sister, Rocky," he replied.

Finally calming down enough so that I could think straight, we headed to the hospital. Kamari's phone was blowing up the entire time. When he answered, it was Kairo on the other end. He was talking calm, like he didn't know what was going on and that seemed odd to me. Here I was in panic mode and he was just as cool as he could be.

"What y'all doing?" he asked.

"On the way to the hospital to check on Asha?" Kamari asked.

"Ight, Tez didn't say anything about who did it?" he questioned.

"He was talking so fast. I could barely make out what he was saying," Kamari responded.

As we pulled up to a red light, I pulled out my phone to check Facebook. I knew a couple people were on my page and I knew someone had to film it. Mari was still talking to Kairo on the phone.

"Aye, hold up, bro, some shit isn't right," Kamari said.

"What you see, bro?" Kairo asked.

"Some fucking cars been following me for a lil minute," he replied.

When we came to a complete stop, our car was hit from behind. Before I could blink, the windows of the cars next to us rolled down and started shooting.

"Oh shit, they shooting! Hold on," Kamari said.

As he jumped over to my side to shield me, I knew that he had been hit because he yelled out. It seemed like they were shooting forever before they pulled off. I heard the sirens in the distance so I knew they were close. I could hear Kamari breathing and checked for a pulse, so I knew that he was alive. When the police and ambulance arrived, they pulled him off me and placed him on a stretcher. I jumped into the back of the ambulance and we headed to the hospital. When we arrived at the hospital, everything went black.

BUDAH

This couldn't be fucking happening. My lady, brother, and sis-in-law were all in the same fucking hospital at one time. I was sitting there with Miya, Robi, and Blessing, waiting on news about everyone. As I was waiting, Tez walked in. We dapped it up and walked over to a corner.

"What's good?" I asked.

"Yo, Ameka was fighting Asha and, from what I'm hearing, her mother was in on it too. Asha's homegirl right there was trying to fight them off with her so you might want to go and say something to her," Tez said.

"What the fuck? I know her and her mother don't get down like that but to set her up to get jumped is fucked up. Find her mother, Ameka, and anyone else that has something to do with it. I know them niggas in the hood recorded that shit too. I want all phones that have the videos and I mean every one of them. When you get them all together, take all of them to the warehouse by the water and tie them all up," I responded.

I walked over the chick that was sitting by the soda machine. I saw that Blaze, Snow, and Reese had walked in so I guess they heard the news about Kamari.

"Yo, you Asha's friend?" I asked.

"Yeah, I'm Monica," she replied.

"Well come over here and sit with the family. I appreciate you helping Asha," I replied.

"It's nothing. Asha and I were kicking ass back in middle school so it's only right I knock a couple bitches out for GP," she replied.

As we were walking over to everyone, the doctor came out. "The Family of Asha Gray?"

"Right here!" Aunt Robi called out.

"Hello, I'm Dr. Channing. Ms. Gray sustained an injury to the back of her head and to her back. I believe that it was a bat or something in that shape. When she was hit in the back, one of her ribs were cracked so she will feel pain from that once the meds were off. She doesn't have a concussion but if she experiences blurriness, sensitivity to sunlight or anything like that, bring her back. She also has about ten stitches in her head. She will have to come back to have those removed or see her family doctor."

"Thank you. When can we see her?" Aunt Robi asked.

"I can take two back right now," he responded.

"Go head back, Robi. I'll be back after I talk to the fellas," I responded.

Once she went back with Monica, I went outside to the parking garage where all the bosses were waiting on me.

"What's up, Budah?" one of the asked.

"Today is the day that the bloodshed will begin for the next seven days. I almost lost the lives of my loved ones because motherfuckers think that it's a game. I know for a fucking fact that we have at least three people that are C.I's to the cops and they will be dealt with the way I see fit. I gave everyone of y'all a chance to clean your house and it fell on deaf ears. Blaze and Tez will give each one of you an assignment that will be carried out. Motherfuckers will feel my wrath by the time that I am finished, and it won't stop until I'm satisfied. Right now, I must go back and check on my family. Dismissed," I stated

When I walked back into the hospital, I went back to check on Asha. Her clothes were bloody and her hair was matted from the blood. When she saw me, it was a mixture of tears and anger.

"You alright, ma?" I asked, kissing her forehead.

"Yeah, can we get out of here?" she asked.

"I can have Robi take you home, but I can't leave," I stated.

"Why not?" she asked.

"Mari and Justice are here," I announced.

'WHAT DO YOU MEAN THEY ARE HERE?" she shouted.

"They were shot at. I'm waiting to hear what is going on with them. I haven't heard anything from the doctors yet," I replied.

"Okay, well let's go find out what's going on with them. What I look like going home when they are still here?" she responded. "Monica, you're still here? I thought you would've left," she said.

"Nah, I'm right here. I called my brother to go and pick up my daughter," Monica replied.

I just knew that she was going to curse my ass out, and I might not even be in the clear because she was too calm with the information she just learned. The entire time that she was talking to Monica, she was cutting her eyes at me and rolling them. I felt helpless that my baby brother was in the hospital and I couldn't get any information from no one.

When we made it to the emergency waiting room, Asha went into complete bitch mode.

"Excuse me, can someone tell me what the fuck is going in with my sister and my brother-in-law? We have been waiting too fucking long and no one has said shit yet!" she shouted.

"Ma'am, I'm going to need you to calm down," the nurse said.

"Oh, I am calm. Now you can get someone out here or I will be walking through those doors and getting answers myself," she stated.

While she was going off, I couldn't even be mad at her because she was right. I called my OG and gave him the latest, and he told me that he and his brothers would be here in a couple of hours.

I had been cool long enough. It was now time for me to start wrecking shit again. Niggas didn't know that I could give a fuck about having mothers, sisters, and babies or anyone else in all black, selling dinners to pay for a fucking funeral. They wanted a war. Well, now they had one. I hoped they were ready because I stayed ready. SAY HELLO TO THE BAD GUY!

TO BE CONTINUED!

Coming 02/20!

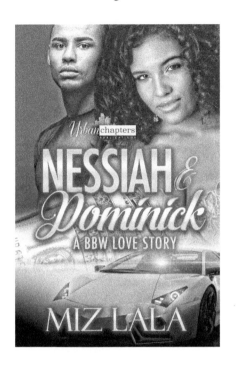

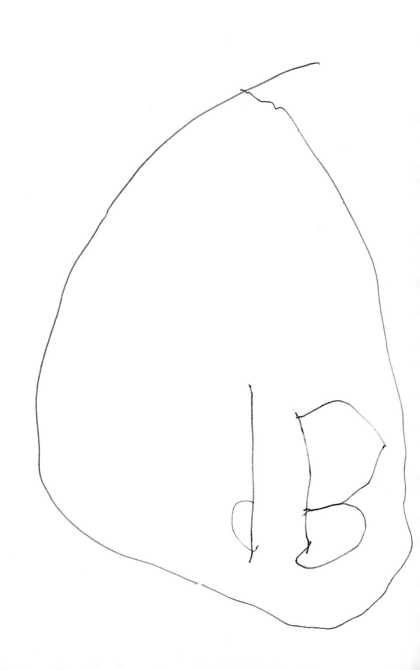

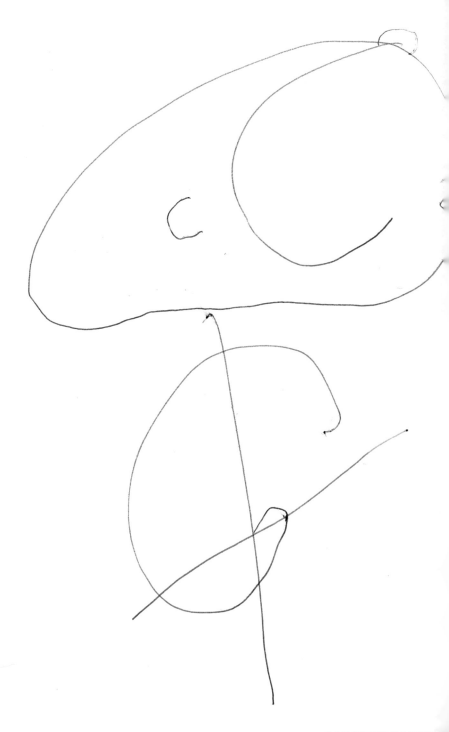

CPSIA information can be obtained
at www.ICGtesting.com
Printed in the USA
LVHW111753120319
610380LV00004B/483/P